DEMCO

NOT
QUITE
KOSHER

BY STUART M. KAMINSKY

Abe Lieberman Mysteries

Lieberman's Folly
Lieberman's Choice
Lieberman's Day
Lieberman's Thief
Lieberman's Law
The Big Silence
Not Quite Kosher

Toby Peters Mysteries

Bullet for a Star
Murder on the Yellow Brick Road
You Bet Your Life
The Howard Hughes Affair
Never Cross a Vampire
High Midnight
Catch a Falling Clown
He Done Her Wrong
The Fala Factor
Down for the Count
The Man Who Shot Lewis Vance
Smart Moves
Think Fast, Mr. Peters
Buried Caesars
Poor Butterfly
The Melting Clock
The Devil Met a Lady
Tomorrow Is Another Day
Dancing in the Dark
A Fatal Glass of Beer

Lew Fonesca Mysteries

Vengeance

Porfiry Rostnikov Novels

Death of a Dissident
Black Knight in Red Square
Red Chameleon
A Cold, Red Sunrise
A Fine Red Rain
Rostnikov's Vacation
The Man Who Walked Like a Bear
Death of a Russian Priest
Hard Currency
Blood and Rubles
Tarnished Icons
The Dog Who Bit a Policeman

Nonseries Novels

When the Dark Man Calls
Exercise in Terror

Biographies

Don Siegel: Director
Clint Eastwood
John Huston, Maker of Magic
Coop: The Life and Legend of Gary Cooper

Other Nonfiction

American Film Genres
American Television Genres
  (with Jeffrey Mahan)
Basic Filmmaking
  (with Dana Hodgdon)
Writing for Television
  (with Mark Walker)

NOT QUITE KOSHER

AN ABE LIEBERMAN MYSTERY

STUART M. KAMINSKY

 FORGE®

A TOM DOHERTY ASSOCIATES BOOK
NEW YORK

NOT QUITE KOSHER: AN ABE LIEBERMAN MYSTERY

A Forge Book
Published by Tom Doherty Associates, LLC
175 Fifth Avenue
New York, NY 10010

www.tor.com

Forge® is a registered trademark of Tom Doherty Associates, LLC.

ISBN: 0-312-87453-7

First Edition: December 2002

Printed in the United States of America

0 9 8 7 6 5 4 3 2 1

TO PETER, RIE, MOLLY,
AND NICHOLAS WITH LOVE

11/02

"Terror holds me, excessive fear. Flights of wandering profit not. Father, I am spent by fear."

—Aeschylus, *The Suppliant Maidens*

NOT
QUITE
KOSHER

"You sure?"

Wychovski looked at Pryor, and said, "I'm sure. One year ago. This day. That jewelry store. It's in my book."

Pryor was short, thin, nervous. Dustin Hoffman on some kind of speed produced by his own body. His face was flat, scarred from too many losses in the ring for too many years. He was stupid. Born that way. Punches to the head hadn't made his IQ rise. But Pryor did what he was told, and Wychovski liked telling Pryor what to do. Talking to Pryor was like thinking out loud.

"One year ago. In your book," Pryor said, looking at the jewelry store through the car window.

"In my book," Wychovski said, patting the right pocket of his black zipper jacket.

"And this is . . . ? I mean, where are we?"

"Northbrook. It's a suburb of Chicago," said Wychovski patiently. "North of Chicago."

Pryor nodded as if he understood. He didn't really, but if Wychovski said so, it must be so. He looked at Wychovski, who sat behind the wheel, his eyes fixed on the door of the jewelry store. Wychovski was broad-shouldered, well built from three years with the weights in Stateville and keeping it up when he was outside. He was nearing fifty, blue eyes, short, short haircut, gray-black hair. He looked like a linebacker, a short linebacker. Wychovski had never played football. He had robbed two Cincinnati Bengals once outside a bar, but that was the closest he got to the real thing. Didn't watch sports on the tube. In prison he had read, wore glasses. Classics. For over a year. Dickens, Poe, Hemingway. Steinbeck. Shakespeare. Freud. Shaw, Irwin and George Bernard. Ibsen, Remarque. Memorized passages. Fell asleep remembering them when the lights went out. Then two years to the day he started, Wychovski stopped reading. Wychovski kept track of time.

Now, Wychovski liked to keep moving. Buy clothes, eat well, stay in classy hotels when he could. Wychovski was putting the cash away for the day he'd feel like retiring. He couldn't imagine that day.

"Tell me again why we're hitting it exactly a year after we hit it before," Pryor said.

Wychovski checked his watch. Dusk. Almost closing time. The couple who owned and ran the place were always the last ones in the mall besides the Chinese restaurant to close. On one side of the jewelry store, Gortman's Jewelry and Fine Watches, was a storefront insurance office. State Farm. Frederick White the agent. He had locked up and gone home. On the other side, Himmell's Gifts. Stuff that looked like it would break if you touched it in the window. Glassy-looking birds and horses. Glassy not classy. Wychovski liked touching real class, like really thin glass wineglasses. If he settled down, he'd buy a few, have a drink every night, run his finger around the rim and make that ringing sound. He didn't know how to do that. He'd learn.

"What?"

"Why are we here again?" Pryor asked.

"Anniversary. Our first big score. Good luck. Maybe. It just feels right."

"What did we get last time?"

The small strip mall was almost empty now. Maybe four cars if you didn't count the eight parked all the way down at the end by the Chinese restaurant. Wychovski could take or leave Chinese food, but he liked the buffet idea. Thai food. That was his choice. Tonight they'd have Thai. Tomorrow they'd take the watches, bracelets, rings to Walter on Polk Street. Walter would look everything over, make an offer. Wychovski would take it. Thai food. That was the ticket.

"We got six thousand last time," Wychovski said. "Five minutes' work. Six thousand dollars. More than a thousand a minute."

"More than a thousand a minute," Pryor echoed.

"Celebration," said Wychovski. "This is a celebration. Back where our good luck started."

"Back light went out," Pryor said, looking at the jewelry store.

"We're moving," Wychovski answered, getting quickly out of the car.

They moved right toward the door. Wychovski had a Glock. His treasure. Read about it in a spy story in a magazine. Had to have it. Pryor had a piece of crap street gun with tape on the handle. Revolver. Six or seven shots. Piece of crap, but a bullet from it would hurt going in and might never come out. People didn't care. You put a gun in their face, they didn't care if it was precision or zip. They knew it could blow out their lights.

Wychovski glanced at Pryor keeping pace at his side. Pryor had dressed up for the job. He had gone through his bag at the motel, asked Wychovski what he should wear. Always asked Wychovski. Asked him if he should brush his teeth. Well, maybe not quite, but asked him almost everything. The distance to the moon. Could eating Equal really give you cancer. Wychovski always had an answer. Quick, ready. Right or wrong. He had an answer.

Pryor was wearing blue slacks and a Tommy Hilfiger blue pullover short-sleeved shirt. He had brushed his hair, polished his shoes. He was ready. Ugly and ready.

Just as the couple inside turned off their light, Wychovski opened the door and pulled out his gun. Pryor did the same. They didn't wear masks, only hit smaller marks that lacked surveillance cameras, like this Dick and Jane little jewelry store. Artists' sketches were for shit. Ski masks itched. Sometimes Wychovski wore dark glasses. That's if they were working the day. Sometimes he had a Band-Aid on his cheek. Let them remember that or the fake mole he got from Gibson's Magic Shop in Paris, Texas. That was a bad hit. No more magic shops. He had scooped up a shopping bag of tricks and practical jokes. Fake dog shit. Fake snot you could hang from your nose. Threw it all away. Kept the mole. Didn't have it on now.

"Don't move," he said.

The couple didn't move. The man was younger than Wychovski by a decade. Average height. He had grown a beard in the last year. Looked older. Wearing a zipper jacket. Blue. Wychovski's was black. Wychovski's favorite colors were black and white.

The woman was blonde, somewhere in her thirties, sort of pretty, too thin for Wychovski's tastes. Pryor remembered the women. He never touched them, but he remembered and talked about them at night in the hotels or motels. Stealing from good-looking women was a high for Pryor. That and good kosher hot dogs. Chicago was always good for hot dogs if you knew where to go. Wychovski knew. On the way back, they'd stop at a place he knew on Dempster in Chicago. Make Pryor happy. Sit and eat a big kosher or two, lots of fries, ketchup, onions, hot peppers. Let Pryor talk about the woman.

She looked different. She was wearing a green dress. She was pregnant. That was it.

"No," she said.

"Yes," said Wychovski. "You know what to do. Stand quiet. No alarms. No crying. Nothing stupid. Boy or a girl?"

Pryor was behind the glass counters, opening them quickly, shoveling, clinking, into the Barnes & Noble bag he had taken from his back pocket. There was a picture of Sigmund Freud on the bag. Sigmund Freud was watching Wychovski. Wychovski wondered what Freud was thinking.

"Boy or girl?" Wychovski repeated. "You know if it's going to be a boy or a girl?"

"Girl," said the man.

"You got a name picked out?"

"Jessica," said the woman.

Wychovski shook his head no and said, "Too . . . I don't know . . . too what everybody else is doing. Something simple. Joan. Molly. Agnes. The simple is different. Hurry it up," he called to Pryor.

"Hurry it up, right," Pryor answered, moving faster, the B&N bag bulging. Freud looking a little plump and not so serious now.

"We'll think about it," the man said.

Wychovski didn't think so.

"Why us?" the woman said. Anger. Tears were coming. "Why do you keep coming back to us?"

"Only the second time," said Wychovski. "Anniversary. One year ago today. Did you forget?"

"I remembered," said the man, moving to his wife and putting his arm around her.

"We won't be back," Wychovski said, as Pryor moved across the carpeting to the second showcase.

"It doesn't matter," said the man. "After this we won't be able to get insurance."

"Sorry," said Wychovski. "How's business been?"

"Slow," said the man, with a shrug. The pregnant woman's eyes were closed.

Pryor scooped.

"You make any of this stuff?" Wychovski asked, looking around. "Last time there were some gold things, little animals, shapes, birds, fish, bears. Little."

"I made those," the man said.

"See any little animals, gold?" Wychovski called to Pryor.

"Don't know," said Pryor. "Just scooping. Wait. Yeah, I see some. A whole bunch."

Wychovski looked at his watch. He remembered where he got it. Right here. One year ago. He held up the watch to show the man and woman.

"Recognize it," he said.

The man nodded.

"Keeps great time," said Wychovski. "Class."

"You have good taste," the man said sarcastically.

"Thanks," said Wychovski, ignoring the sarcasm. The man had a right. He was being robbed. He was going out of business. This was a going out of business nonsale. The man wasn't old. He could start again, work for someone else. He made nice little gold animals. He was going to be a father. The watch told Wychovski that they had been here four minutes.

"Let's go," he called to Pryor.

"One more minute. Two more. Should I look in the back?"

Wychovski hesitated.

"Anything back there?" Wychovski asked the man.

The man didn't answer.

"Forget it," he called to Pryor. "We've got enough."

Pryor came out from behind the case. B&N bag bulging. More than they got the last time. Then Pryor tripped. It happens. Pryor tripped. The bag fell on the floor. Gold and time went flying, a snow or rain of gold and silver, platinum and rings. Glittering, gleaming little animals, a Noah's ark of perfect beasts. And Pryor's gun went off as he fell.

The bullet hit the man in the back. The woman screamed. The man went to his knees. His teeth were clenched. Nice white teeth. Wychovski wondered if such nice white teeth could be real. The woman went down with the man, trying to hold him up.

Pryor looked at them, looked at Wychovski, and started to throw things back in the bag. Wait. That wasn't Freud. Wychovski tried to remember who it was. Not Freud. George Bernard Shaw. It was George Bernard Shaw with wrinkled brow looking at Wychovski, displeased.

"An accident," Wychovski told the woman, who was holding her husband, who now bit his lower lip hard. Blood from the bite. Wychovski didn't want to know what the man's back looked like or where the bullet had traveled inside his body. "Call an ambulance. Nine-one-one. We never shot anybody before. An accident."

Wychovski knelt and began to scoop up watches and the little gold animals from the floor. He stuffed them in his right pocket. He stuffed them in his left and in his right. A few in the pocket of his shirt.

It was more than five minutes now. Pryor was breathing hard trying to get everything. On his knees, scampering like a crazy dog.

"Put the gun away," Wychovski said. "Use both hands. Hurry up. These people need a doctor."

Pryor nodded, put the gun in his pocket and gathered glittering crops. The man had fallen, collapsed on his back. The woman looked at Wychovski, crying. Wychovski didn't want her to lose her baby.

"He have insurance?" he asked.

She looked at him bewildered.

"Life insurance?" Wychovski explained.

"Done," said Pryor with a smile. His teeth were small, yellow.

The woman didn't answer the question. Pryor ran to the door. He didn't look back at what he had done.

"Nine-one-one," Wychovski said, backing out of the store.

Pryor looked both ways and headed for the car. Wychovski was a foot out the door. He turned and went back in.

"Sorry," he said. "It was an accident."

"Get out," the woman screamed. "Go away. Go away. Go away."

She started to get up. Maybe she was crazy enough to attack him. Maybe Wychovski would have to shoot her. He didn't think he could shoot a pregnant woman.

"Joan," he said, stepping outside again. "Joan's a good name. Think about it. Consider it."

"Get out," the woman screamed.

Wychovski got out. Pryor was already in the car. Wychovski ran. Some people were coming out of the Chinese restaurant. Two guys in baseball hats. From this distance, about forty yards, they looked like truckers. There weren't any trucks in the lot. They were looking right at Wychovski. Wychovski realized he was holding his gun. Wychovski could hear the woman screaming. The truckers could probably hear her, too. He ran to the car, got behind the wheel. Pryor couldn't drive, never learned, never tried.

Wychovski shot out of the parking lot. They'd need another car. Not a problem. Night. Good neighborhood. In and gone in something not too new. Dump it. No prints. Later buy a five-year-old GEO, Honda, something like that. Legal. In Wychovski's name.

"We got a lot," Pryor said happily.

"You shot that guy," Wychovski said, staying inside the speed limit, heading for the expressway. "He might die."

"What?" asked Pryor.

"You shot that man," Wychovski repeated, passing a guy in a blue BMW. The guy was smoking a cigarette. Wychovski didn't smoke. He made Pryor stop when they'd gotten together. Inside. In Stateville, he was in a cell with two guys who smoked. Smell had been everywhere. On

Wychovski's clothes. On the pages of his books.

People killed themselves. Alcohol, drugs, smoking, eating crap that told the blood going to their heart that this was their territory now and there was no way they were getting by without surgery.

"People stink," said Wychovski.

Pryor was poking through the bag. He nodded in agreement. He was smiling.

"What if he dies?" Wychovski said.

"Who?"

"The guy you shot," said Wychovski. "Shot full of holes by someone she knows."

The expressway was straight ahead. Wychovski could see the stoplight, the big green sign.

"I don't know her," Pryor said. "Never saw her before."

"One year ago," Wychovski said.

"So? We don't go back. The guy dies. Everybody dies. You said so," Pryor said, feeling proud of himself, holding G.B. Shaw to his bosom. "We stopping for hot dogs? That place you said? Kosher. Juicy."

"I don't feel like hot dogs," said Wychovski.

He turned onto the expressway, headed south toward Chicago. Jammed. Rush hour. Line from here to forever. Moving maybe five, ten miles an hour. Wychovski turned on the radio and looked in the rearview mirror. Cars were lined up behind him. A long showroom of whatever you might want. Lights on, creeping, crawling. Should have stayed off the expressway. Too late now. Listen to the news, music, voices that made sense besides his own. An insulting talk show host would be fine.

"More than we got last time," Pryor said happily.

"Yeah," said Wychovski.

"A couple of hot dogs would be good," said Pryor. "Celebrate."

"Celebrate what?"

"Anniversary. We've got a present."

Pryor held up the bag. It looked heavy. Wychovski grunted. What the hell. They had to eat.

"Hot dogs," Wychovski said.

"Yup," said Pryor.

Traffic crawled. The car in front of Wychovski had a bumper sticker:

DON'T BLAME ME. I VOTED LIBERTARIAN.

What the hell was that? Libertarian. Wychovski willed the cars to move. He couldn't do magic. A voice on the radio said something about Syria. Syria didn't exist for Wychovski. Syria, Lebanon, Israel, Bosnia. You name it. It didn't really exist. Nothing existed. No place existed until it was right there to be touched, looked at, held up with a Glock in your hand.

GLUCK, GLUCK, GLUCK, GLUCK, GLUCK.

Wychovski heard it over the sound of running engines and a horn here and there from someone in a hurry to get somewhere in a hurry. He looked up. Helicopter. Traffic watch from a radio or television station? No. It was low. Cops. The truckers from the Chinese restaurant? Still digesting their fried won ton when they went to their radios or a pay phone or a cell phone or pulled out a rocket.

Cops were looking for a certain car. Must be hundreds, thousands out here. Find Waldo only harder. Wychovski looked in his rearview mirror. No flashing lights. He looked up the embankment to his right. Access drive. The tops of cars. No lights flashing. No uniforms dashing. No dogs barking. Just GLUCK, GLUCK, GLUCK. Then a light.

Pure white circle down on the cars in front. Sweeping right to left, left to right. Pryor had no clue. He was lost in Rolexes and dreams of French fries.

Did the light linger on them? Imagination? Maybe. Description from the hot-and-sour soup-belching truckers? Description from the lady with the baby she was going to name Jessica when Joan would have been better. Joan was Wychovski's mother's name. He hadn't suggested it lightly.

So they had his description. Stocky guy with short gray hair, about fifty, wearing a black zipper jacket. Skinny guy carrying a canvas bag filled with goodies. A jackpot pinata, a heist from St. Nick.

Traffic moved, not wisely or well, but it moved, inched. Music of another time. Tony Bennett? No, hell no. Johnny Mathis singing "Chances Are." Should have been Tommy Edwards.

"Let's go. Let's go," Wychovski whispered to the car ahead.

"Huh?" asked Pryor.

"There's a cop in a helicopter up there," Wychovski said, looking up, moving forward as if he were on the roller-coaster ride creeping toward the top where they would plunge straight down into despair and black air. "I think he's looking for us."

Pryor looked at him, then rolled down his window to stick his head out before Wychovski could stop him.

"Stop that shit," Wychovski shouted, pulling the skinny Pryor inside.

"I saw it," said Pryor.

"Did he see you?"

"No one waved or nothing," said Pryor. "There he goes."

The helicopter roared forward low, ahead of them. Should he take the next exit? Stay in the crowd? And then the traffic started to move a little faster. Not fast, mind you, but it was moving now. Maybe twenty miles an hour. Actually, nineteen, but close enough. Wychovski decided to grit it out. He turned off the radio.

They made it to Dempster in thirty-five minutes and headed east, toward Lake Michigan. No helicopter. It was still early. Too early for an easy car swap, but it couldn't be helped. Helicopters. He searched this way and that, let his instincts take over at a street across from a park. Three-story apartment buildings. Lots of traffic. He drove in a block. Cars on both sides, some facing the wrong way.

"What are we doing?" asked Pryor.

"*We* are doing nothing," Wychovski said. "*I* am looking for a car. I steal cars. I rob stores. I don't shoot people. I show my gun. They show respect. You show that piece of shit in your pocket, trip over thin air, and shoot a guy in the back."

"Accident," said Pryor.

"My ass," said Wychovski. And then, "That one."

He was looking at a gray Nissan a couple of years old parked under a big tree with branches sticking out over the street. No traffic. Dead-end street.

"Wipe it down," Wychovski ordered, parking the car and getting out.

Pryor started wiping the car for prints. First inside. Then outside. By the time he was done, Wychovski had the Nissan humming. Pryor got in the passenger seat, his bag on his lap, going on a vacation. All he needed was a beach and a towel.

They hit the hot dog place fifteen minutes later. They

followed the smell and went in. There was a line. Soft, poppy seed buns. Kosher dogs. Big slices of new pickle. Salty brown fries. They were in line. Two women in front of them were talking. A mother and daughter. Both wearing shorts and showing stomach. Pryor looked back at the door. He could see the Nissan. The bag was in the trunk, with George Bernard Shaw standing guard.

The woman and the girl were talking about Paris. Plaster of? Texas? Europe? Somebody they knew? Nice voices. Wychovski tried to remember when he had last been with a woman. Not that long ago. Two months? Amarillo? Las Vegas? Moline, Illinois?

It was their turn. The kid in the white apron behind the counter wiped his hands, and said, "What can I do for you?"

You can bring back the dead, thought Wychovski. You can make us invisible. You can teleport us to my Aunt Elaine's in Corpus Christi.

"You can give us each a hot dog with the works," Wychovski said.

"Two for me," said Pryor. "And fries."

"Two for both of us. Lots of mustard. Grilled onions. Tomatoes. Cokes. Diet for me. Regular for him."

The mother and daughter were sitting on stools, still talking about Paris and eating.

"You got a phone?" Wychovski asked, paying for their order.

"Back there," said the kid, taking the money.

"I'm going back there to call Walter. Find us a seat where we can watch the car."

Pryor nodded and moved to the pickup order line. Wychovski went back there to make the call. The phone was next to the toilet. He used the toilet first and looked at himself in the mirror. He didn't look good. Decidedly.

He filled the sink with water, cold water, and plunged his face in. Maybe the sink was dirty? Least of his worries. He pulled his head out and looked at himself. Dripping wet reflection. The world hadn't changed. He dried his face and hands and went to the phone. He had a calling card, AT&T. He called Walter. The conversation went like this.

"Walter? I've good goods."

"Jewelry store?"

"It matters?"

"Matters. Cops moved fast. Man's in the hospital maybe dying. Church deacon or something. A saint. All over television, with descriptions of two dummies I thought I might recognize."

"Goods are goods," said Wychovski.

"These goods could make a man an accessory maybe to murder. Keep your goods. Take them who knows where. Get out of town before it's too late, my dear. You know what I'm saying?"

"Walter, be reasonable."

"My middle name is reasonable. It should be 'careful' but it's 'reasonable.' I'm hanging up. I don't know who you are. I think you got the wrong number."

He hung up. Wychovski looked at the phone and thought. St. Louis. There was a guy, Tanner, in St. Louis. No, East St. Louis. A black guy who'd treat them fair for their goods. And Wychovski had a safe deposit box in St. Louis with a little over sixty thousand in it. They'd check out of the motel and head for St. Louis. Not enough cash with them without selling the goods or going to the bank to get a new car. They'd have to drive the Nissan, slow and easy. All night. Get to Tanner first thing in the morning when the sun was coming up through the Arch.

Wychovski went down the narrow corridor. Cardboard boxes made it narrower. When he got to the counter, the mother and daughter were still eating and talking and drinking. Lots of people were. Standing at the counters or sitting on high stools with red seats that swirled. Smelled fantastic. Things would be alright. Pryor had a place by the window, where he could watch the car. He had finished one hot dog and was working on another. Wychovski inched in next to him.

"We're going to St. Louis," he said behind a wall of other conversations.

"Okay," said Pryor, mustard on his nose. No questions. Just "okay."

Then it happened. It always happens. Shit always happens. A cop car, black-and-white, pulled into the lot outside the hot dog place. It was a narrow lot. The cops were moving slowly. Were they looking for a space and a quick burger or hot dog? Were they looking for a stolen Nissan?

The cops stopped next to the Nissan.

"No," moaned Pryor.

Wychovski grabbed the little guy's arm. The cops turned toward the hot dog shop window. Wychovski looked at the wall, ate his dog, and ate slowly, his heart going mad. Maybe he'd die now of a heart attack. Why not? His father had died on a Washington, D.C., subway just like that.

Pryor was openly watching the cops move toward them.

"Don't look at them," Wychovski whispered. "Look at me. Talk. Say something. Smile. I'll nod. Say anything."

"Are they coming for us?" asked Pryor, working on his second dog.

"You've got mustard on your nose. You want to go down with mustard on your nose? You want to be a joke on the ten o'clock news?"

Wychovski took a napkin and wiped Pryor's nose as the cops came in the door and looked around.

"Reach in your pocket," said Wychovski. "Take out your gun. I'm going to do the same. Aim it at the cops. Don't shoot. Don't speak. If they pull out their guns, just drop yours. It'll be over, and we can go pray that the guy you shot doesn't die."

"I don't pray," said Pryor, as the cops, both young and in uniform, moved through the line of customers down the middle of the shop, hands on holstered guns.

Wychovski turned, and so did Pryor. Guns out, aimed. Butch and Sundance. A John Woo movie.

"Hold it," shouted Wychovski.

Oh God, I pissed in my pants. Half an hour to the motel. Maybe twenty years to life to the motel.

The cops stopped, hands still on their holsters. The place went dead. Someone screamed. The mother or the daughter who had stopped talking about Paris.

"Let's go," said Wychovski.

Pryor reached back for the last half of his hot dog and his little greasy bag of fries.

"Is that a Glock?" asked the kid behind the counter.

"It's a Glock," said Wychovski.

"Cool gun," said the kid.

The cops didn't speak. Wychovski didn't say anything more. He and Pryor made it to the door, backed away across the parking lot, watching the cops watching them. The cops wouldn't shoot. Too many people.

"Get in," Wychovski said.

Pryor got in the car. Wychovski reached back to open the driver-side door. Hard to keep his gun level at the kid cops and open the door. He did it, got in, started the car, and looked in the rearview. The cops were coming out, guns drawn. There was a barrier in front of him, low, a couple of inches, painted red. Wychovski gunned forward over the barrier. Hell, it wasn't his car, but it was his life. He thought there was just enough room to get between a white minivan and an old convertible who-knows-what.

The cops were saying something. Wychovski wasn't listening. He had pissed in his pants, and he expected to die of a heart attack. He listened for some telltale sign. The underbody of the Nissan caught the red barrier, scraped, and roared over. Wychovski glanced toward Pryor, who had the window open and was leaning out, his piece of crap gun in his hand. Pryor fired as Wychovski made it between minivan and convertible, taking some paint off both sides of the Nissan in the process.

Pryor fired again as Wychovski hit the street. Wychovski heard the hot dog shop's window splatter. He saw one of the young cops convulsing, flapping his arms. Blood. Wychovski and Pryor wouldn't be welcome here in the near future. Then came another shot as Wychovski turned right. This one went through Pryor's face. Through his cheek and back out. He was hanging out the window making sounds like a gutted dog. Wychovski floored the Nissan. He could hear Pryor's head bouncing on the door.

The cop who had not been shot was going for his car, making calls, and Pryor's head was bouncing something out of the jungle on the door. Wychovski made a hard right down a semidark street. He pulled over to the curb. Wychovski grabbed Pryor's shirt, pulled him back through the window, and reached past him to close the door. Pryor was looking up at him with wide surprise.

Wychovski drove. There were lights behind him now, a block back. Sirens. The golden animals lay heavy in his pockets and over his heart. He turned left, wove around. No idea where he was. No one to talk to. Just me and my radio.

Who knows how many minutes later he came to a street called Oakton and headed east, for Sheridan Road, Lake Shore Drive, Lake Michigan. People passed in cars. He passed people walking. People looked at him. The bloody door. That was it. Pryor had marked him. No time to stop and clean it up. Not on the street. He hit Sheridan Road and looked for a place to turn, found it. Little dead end. Black-on-white sign: NO SWIMMING. A park.

He pulled in between a couple of cars he didn't look at, popped the trunk lock, and got out. There was nothing in the trunk but the bag of jewelry. He dumped it all into the trunk, shoved some watches in his pocket, picked up the empty canvas bag, closed the trunk, went around the side to look at Pryor, who was trying to say something but had nothing left to say it with. Wychovski pulled him from the car and went looking for water.

Families were having late picnics. Couples were walking. Wychovski looked for water, dragging, carrying Pryor, ignoring the looks of the night people. He sat Pryor on an empty bench next to a fountain. Pryor sagged and groaned. He soaked George Bernard Shaw and worked on Pryor's face with the bag. It made things worse. He worked, turned the canvas bag. Scrubbed. He went back for more water, wrung the bloody water from the bag. Worked again. Gunga Din. Fetch water. Clean up. Three trips, and it was done. George Bernard Shaw was angry. His face was red under the dim park lamp.

"Stay here," he told Pryor. "I'll be right back."

Wychovski ran to the parking lot, not caring anymore who might be watching, noticing. He opened the trunk and threw the bag in. When he turned, he saw the cop car coming down the street. Only one way in the lot. Only one way out. The same way. He grabbed six or seven more watches and another handful of little golden animals and quickly shoved them in his bulging pockets. Then he moved into the park, off the path, toward the rocks. Last stand? Glock on the rocks? Couldn't be. It couldn't end like this. He was caught between a cop and a hard place. Funny. Couldn't laugh though. He hurried on, looking back to see the cop car enter the little lot.

Wouldn't do to leave Pryor behind unless he was dead. But Pryor wasn't dead.

Wychovski helped him up with one arm and urged him toward the little slice of moon. He found the rocks. Kids were crawling over them. Big rocks. Beyond them the night and the lake like an ocean of darkness, end of the world. Nothingness. He climbed out and down.

Three teenagers or college kids, male, watched him make his way down toward the water with Pryor. Stop looking at us, he willed. Go back to playing with yourselves, telling lies, and being stupid. Just don't look at me. Wychovski crouched behind a rock, pulling the zombie Pryor with him, the water touching his shoes.

He had no plan. Water and rocks. Pockets full of not much. Crawl along the rocks. Get out. Find a car. Drive to the motel. Get to St. Louis. Tanner might give him a few hundred, maybe more for what he had. Start again. No more Pryor. He would find a new Pryor to replace the prior Pryor, a Pryor without a gun.

Wychovski knew he couldn't be alone.

"You see two men out here?" He heard a voice through the sound of the waves.

"Down there," came a slightly younger voice.

Wychovski couldn't swim. Give up or keep going. He pushed Pryor into the water and kept going. A flashlight beam from above now. Another from the direction he had come.

"Stop right there. Turn around and come back the way you came," said a voice.

"He's armed," said another voice.

"Take out your gun and hold it by the barrel. Now."

Wychovski considered. He took out the Glock. Great gun. Took it out slowly, looked up, and decided it was all a what-the-hell life anyway. He grabbed the gun by the handle, holding on to the rock with one hand. He aimed toward the flashlight above him. But the flashlight wasn't aimed at him. It was shining on the floating, flailing Pryor.

Wychovski fell backward. His head hit a jutting rock. Hurt. But the water, the cold water was worst of all.

"Can you get to him, Dave?" someone called frantically.

"I'm trying."

Pryor was floating on his back, bobbing in the black waves. I can float, he thought, looking at the flashlight. Float out to some little sailboat, climb on, get away.

He floated farther away. Pain gone cold.

"Can't reach him."

"Shit. He's floating out. Call it in."

No one was trying to reach Wychovski. There were no lights on him.

Footsteps. Wychovski looked up. On the rocks above him, Wychovski could see people in a line looking down at Pryor as he floated farther and farther from the shore into the blackness. Wychovski looked for the moon and stars. They weren't there.

Maybe the anniversary hit hadn't been such a good idea.

He closed his eyes and thought that he had never fired his Glock, never fired any gun. It was a damned good gun.

Wychovski crawled along the rocks, half in half out of the water.

He looked back. There was no sign or sound of Pryor.

The man sat on a polished light wood bench in the blue-tiled lobby of Temple Mir Shavot, looking at the door. A white-on-black plastic plate told him that beyond the door was the temple office and that of the rabbi. It was a little after eight on a Thursday morning, and he had been sitting for almost forty minutes.

He knew the rabbi was in. He had seen a modest green Mazda in the parking spot of the rabbi and the license plate was marked "clergy." The man had intended to stride in, find the rabbi, and beg him, if necessary, for an immediate meeting. But when he had seen the door, the man hesitated, his legs weak and heavy. He made it to the bench and sat looking first at his shaking hands, then at the door.

From beyond a door to his right, the voices of men came in a low chant. Occasionally, a voice would rise with determination and even emotion. The man, who had not been in a house of worship since he was a child, remembered the morning *minyans* his father and grandfather had taken him to even before he went to school. There was something plaintive and alien in the sound of long-forgotten Hebrew, and the man, who had regained some control of his legs, now felt as if he might begin to weep.

A few people had passed in the time he had been sitting. Most did not look at him. One woman, heavy, young, wearing thick glasses and carrying a stack of yellow flyers, gave him a smile he was unable to return.

He was, he knew, not a memorable man. Average height, not overweight, dark face now in need of a shave, very black wavy hair he had not combed but which he had brushed back and down with his fingers. He wore slacks, a sport jacket, and a tie loose at the collar. His clothes were conservative and unmemorable unless someone looked a little more carefully and noted the wrinkles and the dark irregular splash marks on his jacket and slacks and marks, which were smaller but definitely red, on his white shirt.

He sighed deeply, thinking he recognized the ending of the morning prayers by the required ten men or more who formed the prayer group. He started to rise, not sure whether he was going to leave or go to the door to the office and step in.

He was saved from the decision by the opening of the door. Two men stepped into the lobby. Their voices echoed slightly when they spoke though they were relatively quiet.

One man was large, burly, maybe about fifty and bearing the look of an ex-athlete whose pink face strongly suggested that he was not Jewish. But the man knew that Jews came in all sizes, faces, and colors. The other man was a study in contrast. He was thin, a bit less than average height, and probably nearing seventy. His hair was curly and white, and he had a little mustache equally white. The older man had one of those perpetually sad looks and resembled one of those contrite beagles the waiting man's Uncle Jack had owned.

"Rabbi," said the big man, "I'll be back here with the car in half an hour."

"Make that an hour, Father Murphy," said the smaller man.

The big man looked at his watch, nodded, and said, "That should give me enough time to check on Rabbit."

Both the rabbi and the priest wore little round black *kepuhs* as did the man who watched them. He had remembered to take one out of the box inside the entrance and cover his head in the house of the Lord.

The big priest moved past the waiting man, glanced at him, and went through the door into the morning sunlight. The rabbi turned and started down the hallway.

"Please," called the waiting man.

The rabbi stopped and looked at him.

"Yeah?"

"I . . . can we talk for a few minutes?"

The rabbi looked at his watch and said, "Me?"

"Yes, it's important."

"I know you?"

"No," said the man.

"I've got a meeting in ten minutes," the rabbi said. "What is it?"

The man rose from the bench, touched his forehead and said, "Someplace a little private?"

The rabbi shrugged and held out his hand toward white double doors across the lobby. The man followed as the rabbi opened a door and stepped into a huge carpeted room with three-story ceilings and stained-glass windows. There were wooden benches facing the platform, the *be-*

mah, and on the *bemah* were a podium on the left and a table on the right. Built into the wall behind podium and table was a tall curtained ark, which the man remembered contained at least one Torah, a carefully handwritten scroll containing the first five books of the Scriptures.

It all came back to him. Genesis, Exodus, Numbers, Deuteronomy, Leviticus. Hebrew words without meaning came rushing into his consciousness from the well of memory. He touched his forehead. He had not slept at all.

There were folding chairs neatly stacked against the back wall. The rabbi motioned for the man to follow him and unfolded two chairs facing each other in the back of the room. They sat. The rabbi put his hands in his lap and waited.

"I was born a Jew," the man said. "When I got married, my wife is Catholic, I converted. I don't know if I'm still a Jew."

"Tough question. As far as I'm concerned, you're born a Jew, you're a Jew forever. Maybe you can be both, like dual citizenship."

"So, I'm in the right place," the man said, whispering.

"Depends on what's on your mind."

"Confession," the man said. "Isn't a rabbi sort of like a priest? I mean, if something is told to a rabbi in confidence, if someone confesses to something, is it protected? Is the rabbi forbidden to tell anyone?"

"Depends on the rabbi."

"What about here? This synagogue?"

"The rabbi wouldn't tell anyone."

The man sighed.

"My name is Arnold Sokol. I killed a boy last night. I think I killed a boy last night."

"Who?"

"I don't know," said Sokol touching his forehead. "Mary, my wife, and I had a fight. The minute I came home from work. I worked late last night. You know the Hollywood Linen Shop in Old Orchard?"

"No."

"That's my family's. Where was . . . Oh, yes. Mary and I we've been having a lot of them, fights. I don't go to church with her. She wants more children. We've got two. I said, 'no more.' Fight. No hitting, nothing like that. Just anger, shouting. You know, I said I gave up my religion for you, and she said she gave up friends and family and since when had I practiced any religion. The kids were in bed, but I'm sure they heard the whole thing. Mary got loud. I got loud. The baby cried. I went out."

"Out?"

"For a drive. It was about eleven. We live in the city, on Sheridan, near Loyola University. I drove to the lake, in Evanston, near Northwestern University. I sat on the rocks listening to the waves. I had a lot on my mind. Business. Mary and I haven't been getting along. It's my fault. She's educated. An MBA. Runs her own business out of the apartment. I made it through high school."

"What happened by the lake?"

"It started."

"It?"

"I guess they spotted me alone. I didn't hear them coming." Sokol went on looking toward the ark.

"How many?"

"Three. Young. White. I don't think any of them was more than eighteen, maybe a little older, maybe. I didn't know they were there till one of them behind me said,

'Hey, you.' I was startled. I turned around and saw them, standing in a line on the grass behind the rocks. They were smiling. I looked around. We were the only ones in sight. I thought about running, jumping into the water, shouting, but I knew none of them would work. And I didn't consider fighting. I exercise a little, but . . . I've never been in a real fight, even when I was a kid."

"What did they say, do?"

"One of them said, 'How'd you like to give us your watch and wallet?' Another one said, 'And your belt.' And a third one, the biggest one, a blond with short hair said, "And anything else you've got in your pockets." I stood up. The strange thing was that I wasn't afraid. I had fought with Mary. I was depressed. So many things have . . . One of them said, 'Come here.' I stayed on the rocks. Maybe deep inside I was afraid to move, but I didn't feel afraid. I didn't even consider calling for the help of God, and certainly not to Jesus. This is a confession, right?"

"Sounds like one to me," said the rabbi.

"I've been a lousy Catholic," said Arnold Sokol. "I don't believe. I did it to please my wife. Is that a sin? I mean for a Jew?"

"A mistake maybe, not a sin. Least I don't think so. That's between you and God," said the rabbi.

"But I don't believe in God either. They came toward me. I was wearing these shoes, good shoes for standing all day. Not good for running on rocks. One of them came alone. I think he was the leader. He held out his hand. He was smiling. One of the other boys was looking around to see if anyone was coming. The one in front of me said, 'Give fast, man.' I was frozen. I thought they were going to beat me, probably kill me. When he punched me in the face, I stumbled back, almost losing my balance. He came forward. One of the others, I don't know which, said, 'Hurry up, Z,' something like that. The one called Z came at me. I didn't know what was behind. Something happened inside me. I don't know what. Rage, fear. Humiliation. I grabbed his arm and pulled. He didn't expect it. I almost fell again but didn't. The one called Z went down on his face on the edge of a rock. The others stood frozen for a second. Z got to one knee and grabbed me around the waist. I don't know if he wanted my help or to kill me. His head was . . . cut, blood was flowing down his face. In the moonlight . . . I can't describe it. He sat back. The other two came forward. One of them slipped on the rocks and tumbled into the water shouting something obscene at me. The last one, a big blond with short hair, started to punch me. I doubled over and then came up. I hit the one in front of me, the big blond, in the throat. He made a gargling sound, grabbed his throat, and said, 'I'm gonna kill you, mister.'

"I thought I heard the one in the water climbing out. I tried to pull away. The big one hit me here, on the side of my head. That's when I heard the voices. I think it was a group of Northwestern students going back to campus. The one holding me hit me again, harder. I think the bone under my right eye might be broken. Maybe his knuckles are broken. The one in the water had climbed out, and he started for me, hair hanging down, hate in his eyes. 'Help Z,' the one who had hit me said. 'Let's go.' And then he looked at me, and said, 'We'll find you, mister. We'll kill you.' They went away. The one I had hit in the throat was still trying to catch his breath, the one who had said he'd kill me.

"I looked down at the one called Z. It was hard to tell in the moonlight. There was a lot of blood, and he wasn't moving. I went over the rocks back to the grass and stood shaking, my hands on my knees. The group that had saved my life passed on the pathway about thirty yards away. They were too busy talking and possibly a little too drunk to see me. I wandered, drove, and came here."

"That it?" asked the rabbi.

"No," said Sokol, looking at his hands. "I wanted to kill him. I wanted to kill them all. I want to say I'm sorry for what I did, but I'm not. I feel good. I did something. God help me, I may be a murderer, and I feel good about it and bad about it. Am I making sense? Do you understand?"

"I think I understand," said the rabbi.

"I'm not going to the police," Sokol said. "I'm not going to tell Mary. I'm going to think about this. I can kill. Somehow it's made me feel better about myself, what I think about myself. I'll keep this secret. I just had to tell someone."

"It's too late," said the rabbi.

Sokol looked up.

"Too late?"

"You've already gone to the police," the rabbi said.

"What?"

"I'm a police officer. Detective Sergeant Lieberman."

"The priest called you 'Rabbi,' " the confused Sokol said.

"He's not a priest. He's a cop, too," said Lieberman. "We call each other 'Rabbi' and 'Father Murphy.' "

"You lied," said Sokol, angrily rising from the folding chair, which clattered back behind him.

"Never told you I was the rabbi," Lieberman said, still sitting.

"You should have stopped me, told me."

"Maybe," said Lieberman. "I'm not sure what the rules are."

"I could kill you right here," said Sokol, looking around for something to attack the smaller man with. He started for the chair.

"I don't know what the punishment is for killing someone in a synagogue," said Lieberman. "I wouldn't be surprised if God struck you dead. Actually, I would be surprised. On the other hand, I don't know what he would do to me if I had to shoot you."

Sokol had his back turned to Lieberman. He had one hand on the fallen chair when he looked over his shoulder and saw the detective aiming a gun in his direction.

Sokol took his hand away from the chair, faced the detective, and began to cry.

"I'm putting the gun away," said Lieberman. "Shouldn't have brought it in here anyway. You going to give me trouble?"

Sokol shook his head no.

"You want to see Rabbi Wass?"

Again, Sokol shook his head no and tried to keep the tears back.

"Cheer up," said Lieberman, standing. "I'm not sure your confession is admissible."

Someone came through the doors, a youngish man in a suit wearing glasses.

"Lieberman . . ." he began, then saw the crying man, the overturned chair, and the detective.

"Irving," Lieberman said. "I can't make the meeting to-day. I'll make the one tomorrow. Today's is all yours."

The man in the glasses and designer suit and tie looked as if he were going to speak, changed his mind, and left the room. Lieberman shook his head wearily and turned toward the ark. He stood silently for about a minute.

"Are you praying?" asked Sokol.

"Something like that," said Lieberman.

"For me?"

"Not sure," said Lieberman. "Maybe. Maybe for both of us. Maybe that Irving Hamel, who just burst in here, doesn't screw up the meeting. Maybe . . . I don't use words. I don't know if God is listening. Sometimes I think God created the world and everything on it, including us, then left us on our own, went to some other world, tried again. Maybe he comes back to look in on what he left behind. Maybe he doesn't. I like to think he doesn't. If I thought he did, I'd be a little angry that he doesn't say, 'stop.' You understand?"

"I don't know," said Sokol.

"Good. Neither do I. Let's go make some phone calls."

The secretary, Mrs. Gold, had been with Temple Mir Shavot since the days when it was located in Albany Park and Old Rabbi Wass was still a young man. Now Mrs. Gold, a solid citizen of seventy who liked to reminisce with anyone who would listen about the old days on the West Side when she was a girl, considered herself the protector of the Young Rabbi Wass, who was, at forty-five, no longer quite young.

Mrs. Gold was short. Mrs. Gold was plump. Her hair was short and dyed black, and her glasses hung profession-ally at the end of her nose. She had perfected the art of looking over her glasses at strangers in a way that told them she had some doubts about their intentions and origin.

"Can I use the phone in Rachel's office?" asked Lieberman as Mrs. Gold behind her desk looked at the disheveled and bloodstained Arnold Sokol.

"Why not?" asked Mrs. Gold. "Aren't you supposed to be in a meeting?"

"Something came up," said Lieberman.

"You know what'll happen if you're not in that meeting?"

"Chaos," said Lieberman. " 'The sky will fall and cursed night, it will be up to me to set it right.' "

"Shakespeare?" she said, shaking her head.

"Comes from years of insomnia and reading in the bathtub," said Lieberman, motioning for Sokol to follow him into a small office next to the wooden door on which a plaque indicated the office of Rabbi Wass.

Lieberman pointed to a chair next to the desk. Sokol sat while Lieberman stood making calls and taking notes.

A resigned calm had taken over Arnold Sokol. Events would carry him. He would drift. Others would take care of him, possibly send him to prison. He had experienced his moment. It would stay inside. He was complete. He tried to remember every moment of the night before. It came in small, jerking bits in which he stood triumphant. Sokol heard almost nothing of what the detective said, and when Lieberman hung up after taking notes, Sokol had trouble concentrating on what he was being told.

"His name is Zembinsky, Melvin Zembinsky," said Lieberman. "Notice I said 'is.' You didn't kill him. At least he's not dead yet. He's in Evanston Hospital. Let's go see him."

"He's not dead?" asked Sokol. "This is a trick. I killed him. He attacked me. I killed him."

Lieberman looked at the seated man, who looked as if he were going to panic.

"And you want him dead?"

"Yes," said Sokol pounding the desk. "Yes, yes, yes. It's . . . I don't know."

The door to the office opened and a man in a white shirt and dark slacks held up by suspenders stepped in, leaving the door open behind him.

The man was thin, wore glasses and a *kepuh*. He looked at Sokol, then at Lieberman.

"Abraham, what's going on?"

"Rabbi Wass, this is Arnold Sokol. He thought I was you. He confessed to a murder, but the victim isn't dead, and Mr. Sokol is disappointed."

Rabbi Wass looked confused. He took off his glasses, which he often did to make momentary sense of the immediate world, put them on again, and looked at Sokol.

"I was working on my sermon," Rabbi Wass said.

Both Sokol and Lieberman failed to see the relevance of the statement.

"Never mind," said the rabbi. "Who did you try to kill? Why? Why are you disappointed that he isn't dead? And, forgive me, but I don't recognize you. You're not a member of this congregation."

"I'm a Catholic," said Sokol.

"He's a Jew," said Lieberman.

"I thought I killed a young man who was trying to rob me," said Sokol. "Him and his gang, three of them. I fought them off. Then I wanted to confess, to tell someone."

"You were proud of what you had done?" asked the rabbi.

"Yes."

"Why didn't you go to a priest?"

"I . . ."

"He's a Jew, a convert to Catholicism," said Lieberman. "He's as confused as Jerry Slattery."

Slattery was a convert from Catholicism to Judaism. It had come to Slattery when he was fifty. He was a postal worker, a collector of coins, a bachelor with recurrent stomach problems. Then he had become a pain in the behind. No one is more Jewish than a convert. Slattery spoke out, decried the lack of religious discipline in the congregation. He had been to Israel twice, spoke Hebrew almost fluently, and argued with Rabbi Wass on any and all subjects. And then, suddenly, Slattery had second thoughts about his conversion, went to see a priest, and dropped out of religious life of all kinds. He sat at home in his small apartment at night watching television and playing Tetris on a Game Boy.

Rabbi Wass and the priest, Father Sutton at St. Thomas's, had joined forces to save Slattery, had visited him at home, taken him to dinner, tried to argue, persuade, threaten, cajole. So far, nothing had worked, and Lieberman, to tell the truth, was happy that Slattery wasn't around to correct everyone on ritual procedure and rail against the Arab world.

Sokol wasn't a member of the congregation. Sokol was a Catholic. What was Rabbi Wass's obligation, duty? Find the name of the man's priest? Another Slattery situation?

"We're going to the hospital," said Lieberman, motioning for Sokol to rise.

"I'll go with you," said Rabbi Wass. "I'll get my jacket."

"No," said Sokol.

The rabbi paused at the door.

"I would like to go," said the rabbi.

"You can't save my soul," said Sokol. "I don't want it saved, and I don't want clichés and simpleminded advice."

"You'd be surprised at how many people find solace in simple truths," said Rabbi Wass.

"Not me," said Sokol.

"Fine, whatever conversation we have, I'll try to make it dense, metaphysical, and difficult to follow. Will that satisfy you?"

Sokol looked at the rabbi, who was serious and without expression. The rabbi left to get his jacket.

Ten minutes later, Lieberman's partner returned, was briefed, and the four men got into the car and were headed for the hospital.

"I checked with your friend Bryant in Evanston," Lieberman said in the front seat while Hanrahan drove. "Our victim is eighteen, has a long list of arrests for robbery, assault. Did six months as a juvenile offender. Father's a lawyer. Mother's a Realtor and on a state juvenile crime commission."

Hanrahan looked into the rearview mirror. Rabbi Wass was speaking softly to Sokol, who seemed galaxies away.

"What're we doing, Abe? Why not turn him over to Bryant and get to the station before Kearney puts us on report."

"I called Kearney. He was in one of his moods. Doesn't care what we do," said Lieberman.

"It would be a comfort, though a small one, if I had some idea of what we were doing," said Hanrahan, as they drove down the road between the parking structure and the rear of the hospital. Hanrahan parked near the Emergency Room and put down his visor with the Chicago police card clipped to it.

"I think we're trying to save a man's soul, whatever that is," said Lieberman.

"We'd be better off out catching a few bad guys," said Hanrahan.

"I called his wife."

"You got a lot done fast, Rabbi."

"She's coming here. Older kid's in school. She's bringing the baby."

Hanrahan looked in the mirror again.

"Looks like a true believer in nothing," said Hanrahan.

"Maybe," said Lieberman. "Let's go."

They got out of the car, two policemen ahead, the rabbi and suspect behind.

There were about a dozen people in the waiting room, none of them Sokol's wife. They had beaten her there, which was fine with Lieberman. Identification was shown, and the woman behind the counter told them how to get up to the room of Melvin Zembinsky.

At the nursing station, a thin, pretty black nurse with her hair in a bun said that Zembinsky had suffered no serious injury other than facial contusions, a concussion that knocked him out, and a cut in his head that required thirty-two stitches. He needed a few days of tests and observation, but there was no reason they couldn't see him, especially since he was a suspect in a crime.

There were two men in the other beds in the room with Zembinsky. Neither man was in any condition to notice the quartet that moved to the bedside of the bandaged young man whose eyes were closed. Hanrahan pulled the curtain around the bed to give them some sense of privacy.

"Melvin," said Lieberman.

Nothing.

"Z," Lieberman said, and the young man's eyes struggled and opened.

"I'm Detective Lieberman. This is my partner, Detective Hanrahan, and this is Rabbi Wass. I think you know this man."

Zembinsky's eyes turned to Sokol without recognition.

"He's the one who put you in here," said Lieberman. "Wanna just shake hands and be friends?"

Zembinsky's eyes now turned to the thin little detective.

"I didn't think so," said Lieberman. "You're a Jew."

"I'm nothing," Zembinsky whispered. "Religion sucks."

"Sokol," said Lieberman. "It sounds like you and your victim have a lot in common."

"Why didn't you die?" asked Sokol with resignation.

"So I could get out of this bed, find you, and punch a hole in your stomach," said Zembinsky so softly that the four men could hardly hear him. Zembinsky's eyes closed, and he seemed exhausted.

"We're gonna get you, man," Zembinsky went on, eyes still closed.

"We're gonna get you at home, or on the street when you don't know we're coming. And if you've got a family . . ."

Lieberman was at the foot of the bed facing the battered young man. Rabbi Wass stood next to the bed with Hanrahan at his side. Sokol stood next to Lieberman.

And it happened. Arnold Sokol let out an animal snort

of rage, pushed Lieberman against the bed, and grabbed
the detective's weapon from his holster. Lieberman's hip
had caught a metal bar. Pain shot through his side.

"No," said Rabbi Wass, as Sokol aimed the weapon at
the young man on the bed, who opened his eyes, looked
at Arnold, and smiled.

"Put it down, Mr. Sokol," said Hanrahan, whose
weapon was out and pointed at the shaking man with the
gun in his hand.

"No," said Sokol. "I'm going to finish this."

"Go ahead," said the young man in the bed. "I don't
give a crap. You'll make the headlines. My friends won't
have any trouble finding you. Shoot. You'll probably miss
and screw it up again."

"You ever fire a weapon, Arnold?" Lieberman said.

"I'm just going to pull the trigger," said Sokol. "Pull it
and pull it till it's empty or the other policeman shoots me.
You don't understand. It has to be, or I'm nothing."

"First the synagogue, now the hospital," said Lieberman.
"And who the hell knows what you've done to my hip?
And let's not forget that if you shoot him with my gun,
I'm in big trouble. I've got a wife, daughter, two grandchildren, a bar mitzvah to pay for, and I'm near a retirement pension. Shoot him and who knows what I lose. All
you lose is your life."

Sokol looked at the three men around the bed and hesitated.

"I have to," he said. "Don't you see?"

"Be quiet, will you," came the voice of a man in another
bed beyond the curtain. "I'm supposed to, for Christ's
sake, rest here."

"Sorry," said Lieberman.

Sokol aimed the gun at the young man in the bed before him. Hanrahan leveled his weapon.

Before he could move, Rabbi Wass leaned over the young man on the bed and covered him with his body, his back to Sokol.

"Get out of the way," Sokol cried.

The rabbi was eye to eye with the battered man on the bed. The pain of the rabbi's weight was offset by the rabbi's attempt at a reassuring smile.

"No," said Rabbi Wass. "Arnold, give Detective Lieberman his gun back. No lives will be lost here with the possible exception of yours and mine."

"I . . ." Sokol stammered, then screamed, "Get the hell off of him."

"I would like to get the hell of his life off of him," said the rabbi, "but at the moment, one step at a time. This is very uncomfortable, Arnold."

"You people are all crazy," said Sokol. "I'm crazy."

"And I'm calling the damn nurse," came the voice from the other bed.

Lieberman held out his hand. Sokol hesitated and handed him the weapon. Hanrahan slowly put his gun away.

"He did it," croaked Zembinsky, looking into the rabbi's eyes.

Rabbi Wass closed his eyes, let out a puff of air, and stood up on less then firm legs.

"You've got balls," said the young man in the bed struggling for air.

"I'll take that as a compliment," said the rabbi, adjusting his glasses. "Now, if you want to repay me and God for saving your life, promise that this is all ended, that you will not seek revenge. You don't deserve revenge."

The pretty black nurse came in and saw that Zembinsky was having trouble breathing.

"What happened?" she asked, looking at Lieberman and then at her patient, who was breathing loud and heavily.

"I fell upon him," said Rabbi Wass.

The nurse leaned over the heavily breathing young man and said, "You people have some damn weird rituals."

"We do," said Lieberman.

Zembinsky's eyes met those of Arnold Sokol, and he spoke as the nurse listened to his chest with the stethoscope that hung around her neck.

"Okay," the young man gasped. "I owe you one. I leave the bastard alone. He doesn't bring any charges."

"Be quiet," the nurse said.

"Sokol nodded yes and Zembinsky nodded and closed his eyes.

The nurse stood up.

"He'll be alright," she said. "I'd say this visit is over."

"Amen," said Lieberman.

"You believe the little bugger?" asked Hanrahan in the corridor outside the room.

"Yes," said Rabbi Wass.

"I think so," said Sokol.

"Yes," said Lieberman, but kept to himself the knowledge gained from more than thirty years on the street, a knowledge that one's word was only as good as the person who gave it, and rage walked the streets.

"Go downstairs, Arnold Sokol," said Rabbi Wass. "Your wife should be there. Go home. I'll call you if you wish, see how you're doing."

"I . . . I'd . . . That would be fine."

"Maybe you could come back for a service, Friday night? I think you'll be the subject of my sermon. I don't know what I'll say. Maybe I'll surprise us both. God often gives me words I didn't expect. Sometimes they're not so bad."

"I'll think about it," said Sokol, shaking hands with the two policemen.

"I'd say you owe the rabbi," said Hanrahan.

"Yes," said Sokol, looking at his watch. "I could still take a shower, change clothes, and get to work."

"The baby's name?" asked Lieberman, as Sokol started to turn toward the elevator. "What's your baby's name?"

"Luke," said Sokol. "Did I tell you my wife's name is Mary?"

"You did," said Lieberman. "They're waiting for you downstairs."

The three men stood in the hospital corridor while Sokol got in the elevator.

"You're a hero, Rabbi," said Lieberman.

"I'm a man, that's all," said Rabbi Wass.

"So," said Lieberman. "What does it mean? What happened this morning?"

"I don't know," said the rabbi. "But it feels right."

When the three men got down to the lobby, the tattered Arnold Sokol was standing in the corner near the window arguing with a plump woman with disheveled hair and a baby over her shoulder.

"Doesn't look promising," said Hanrahan.

"They're talking," said Rabbi Wass, adjusting his glasses. "It's a start."

Sokol motioned toward them. They couldn't see a way out other than coming over to the family.

"Mary, these people helped me. I don't know their names."

"I'm Rabbi Wass. This is Detective Abraham Lieberman and Detective William Hanrahan. Chicago police."

"Thank you," the woman said, handing the baby to her husband and reaching out her hand.

They each took her hand in turn and watched while the couple moved away.

"Time for coffee?" asked Lieberman.

Why not?" said Rabbi Wass, who walked ahead of them, lost in his thoughts.

"Abe," Hanrahan said softly. "You load your weapon yet this morning?"

"Nope," said Lieberman. "Father Murph, you know I don't load till I get to the squad room."

"Yeah," said Hanrahan, as the automatic doors opened in front of the hospital. "How about you paying for the coffee?"

"How about Rabbi Wass paying for the coffee and Danish?" Lieberman said, as the rabbi stood waiting for them.

"That'll be fine with me," said Hanrahan. "Just fine."

The Pinchuk sisters were seated at the Lieberman dining room table alongside each other, a thick large book that looked like a photograph album in front of them, a black briefcase next to it. At the far end of the table sat Lieberman's grandson Barry. And Lieberman's wife, Bess, standing straight, wearing a black dress and a serious look, sat across from the sisters.

Lieberman did not sigh. He wanted to. He wanted to tell them about the man who had thought he was a rabbi. He wanted to tell them about Rabbi Wass's act of courage. He wanted to tell them he was tired. He wanted to tell them he was hungry.

They were clearly waiting for him as he stepped inside the front door, looked across the darkened living room and into the dining room. Barry looked up at his grandfather, trying to show nothing but seeking a reprieve from the coming ordeal. Lieberman was in no position to grant reprieves.

He took off his shoes, dropped them in the small closet in the tiny alcove, and moved toward the table. He remembered why the Pinchuks, Rose and Esther, were here. He had it in the appointment book in his back pocket. He had chosen to put it from his mind.

"Sorry I'm late," he said, leaning over to kiss Bess on the cheek. His wife was six years younger than Lieberman. She looked at least fifteen years younger and sometimes she looked young enough to be his daughter.

The Liebermans had one daughter, Lisa, and this meeting was a direct result of that offspring.

"Hungry, Abe?" Bess asked.

He had been when he walked through the door, but he did not want to eat in front of the somber Pinchuk girls. Everyone called them "the Pinchuk girls" though Rose was seventy-six and Esther seventy-five. They were both widows. They lived together. They could have passed for twins and wore each other's clothes. The Pinchuk girls were short, looked deceptively frail, wore identical short haircuts for their identical silver hair, and bore the same face as their late mother, which meant they were unblemished and perpetually smiling as if they had a secret and knew how to tolerate even the most outrageous responses the world hurled at them. They were thin female Jewish Buddhas who were about to reveal some of their secrets in their book, briefcase, and memories to Abraham Lieberman.

"I'll eat later. Coffee?"

"I'll get it," said Barry, rising quickly. "We've got some carrot cake, too."

Barry, who was not normally so ready to serve, was almost to the kitchen door. Any respite was welcome, even serving his grandfather.

"No carrot cake for your grandfather."

The Pinchuk sisters had cups of coffee before them. Bess had brought out the good breakfast china Lieberman had gotten for her about five anniversaries ago.

Barry looked at Abe, who shrugged. Abe had a constant battle against cholesterol. God had chosen to torture him by making him love food, especially Jewish food, and then forbidding it to him. Abe had a particular sympathy for the Scriptural Jonah.

"Bring your grandfather the fat-free cookies," said Bess.

Barry went through the door. Lieberman knew his grandson would take as much time as he could get away with before returning.

Abe contemplated the coming fat-free, sugar-free, taste-free cookies that looked like real cookies just as Tarry Radlen, the drug dealer in Albany Park, looked like a real businessman. Better. Radlen's passion was expensive, tasteful clothing. He had neatly trimmed dark hair, gray sideburns, a gentle tan, and an understanding face with bright blue eyes behind stylish Italian glasses.

"Abe," said Bess.

Lieberman came out of his reverie about Tarry Radlen and pursed his lips to stifle the urge to sigh.

"The book," Rose said, putting her left hand on the large white album as if she were about to ask all at the table to swear upon it.

"I see," said Lieberman.

They were there to make arrangements for Barry's coming bar mitzvah. They had six months before that occasion when Barry was to take his place among the men of his religion, was to go through the rituals and be declared a man of Israel who, among other things, could take his place in the morning *minyan*, which required ten Jewish males who had attained manhood through their own bar mitzvahs.

Lieberman well recalled his own bar mitzvah weekend almost fifty years earlier. His own had been, because of his grandfather, an Orthodox ceremony, an ordeal that had caused him endless hours of study, nightmares for months, and, when it was finally over, the greatest sense of relief of his lifetime. Barry's bar mitzvah would be in Temple Mir Shavot with Rabbi Wass and Cantor Fried presiding. Mir Shavot was Conservative. Their joining Mir Shavot had been a compromise many years ago when the old Rabbi Wass was head of the congregation. Lieberman had held out for a Reform congregation, everything in English, a rabbi who played the guitar during services, an occasional reminder that they were Jews, a fact that required no institutional reinforcement for Abraham Lieberman.

But Bess had held out for Mir Shavot, and Lieberman had given in to her wishes as he felt he did in all matters domestic. Which was why he was sitting at the dining room table in West Rogers Park with the Pinchuk sisters who, it seemed, were particularly deferential, not because Lieberman was a policeman but because Bess was President of the Congregation.

"Invitations first," said Esther, looking at the book.

Rose opened the album. The pages faced the Liebermans.

Lieberman had a sudden flashback to his daughter Lisa's bat mitzvah. He had successfully repressed the memory the way, he thought, that women suppressed the pain of childbirth shortly after the agony.

Lisa had been a bright, no, a brilliant and defiant child

of great beauty and will. She had been dragged, primarily by her mother, through the process and performed brilliantly. Lieberman remembered a sense of pride at her performance and a feeling of emotion when Rabbi Wass, Old Rabbi Wass, gave her his blessing. Above all, he remembered two other things. First, the cost. Second, the fact that when he was a boy, girls did not have bat mitzvahs. He did not object to sexual equality, only its cost.

Barry came back in, surprisingly fast, Lieberman thought, and placed coffee and a plate of six cookies next to Abe. Their eyes met. A plea.

"Where's Melisa?" asked Lieberman.

"Upstairs, homework," said Bess.

"I've got a math quiz tomorrow," said Barry, taking his seat at the far end of the not-very-long table.

"Later," said Bess firmly.

"You and Grandpa can make all the decisions," Barry said.

Barry looked remarkably like his father, Todd, who was not seated at this table taking on responsibility for a number of very good reasons. Todd, a professor of classics at Northwestern University, was not Jewish. Todd, whom Lisa had divorced three years earlier, had remarried. Todd, who loved his children and saw them often, far more often than Lisa, who had moved to California, leaving her children with her parents, wanted as little as possible to do with his former wife. Lisa had herself recently remarried, a doctor. A Jewish mother's dream. A decent, warm man. A pathologist. Tall, handsome, had studied in Israel and spoke Hebrew. But there was a catch. With Lisa there was always a catch. Her new husband was black, African-American, Negro, a *shvartze.*

Abe's and Bess's tolerance had been tested, but there had been no doubt about the outcome even before they met Lisa's husband. The Liebermans were in matters social and secular concerned only that the man was decent. He was better than that. Lieberman had grown up in a Chicago West Side ghetto on two sides of which were miles of black families. He had learned then and in later life that race was a test, absurdity, possibly a trial from God if there were a God.

"We are creatures on a small planet," he had explained to Barry and Melisa when they had been told about their mother's new husband. "Our small planet is in a small solar system around a small star. Beyond it are millions of stars, millions upon millions of solar systems. Men and women are one kind of creature on this small planet. We have small differences, different beliefs. The most truly evil man I ever met was black. But then again, the most truly good man I ever met was black. We have better things to do in our time on earth than waste it in battles over which Sneetch on the beach is better than the other."

He had practiced the speech before he had given it. Not in those words exactly, but close, and it had gone well.

He had even told them that there were others, perhaps most people, who didn't see the simple truth of man's insignificance, and that their mother and stepfather were going to have some tough times as they would probably when they were with them.

"Abe," Bess said, touching his arm as he nibbled on a tasteless cookie shaped like a leaf with little green speckles.

"I'm listening," said Lieberman, trying to appear attentive, shifting a little in his chair to ease the slight throbbing in his hip where he had bumped into the bed in Melvin Zembinsky's hospital room.

The bottom line here was that Abe and Bess were going to have to pay for the bar mitzvah. Lisa was willing to come, but she was not willing to pay. It was, she said, a matter of principle. She and God had been at war for the last two decades. The only concessions she would make were that she would attend, be pleasant, and that she and her husband would pay for the flowers on the *bemah*, the platform in the sanctuary on which the services were held. Even that had been her husband's idea.

"How many cards will you need?" Rose asked.

"We have a list," Bess answered, handing an unwrinkled sheet to the Pinchuk sisters. "One hundred and fifty. That includes everyone in Barry's bar mitzvah class, school friends, relatives from New York, California, and St. Louis.

"Most of the out-of-towners won't come," said Lieberman.

"But we're inviting them anyway," Bess said. "We agreed."

"We agreed," Lieberman agreed, picking up his coffee. Barry had prepared it just the way his grandfather liked it, hot with cream and two Equals. He had microwaved the cup so that cream and coffee were hot.

"One hundred and fifty invitations," said Rose, writing in a small black notebook that Lieberman had not noticed before. "Response cards and envelopes. You'll do the addressing?"

"Yes," said Bess.

"You've looked through the book," Esther said, hand flat on the open page. "Have you made a selection?"

"Barry?" Bess asked, looking at her grandson.

Barry shrugged, showing his complete indifference to the selection of cards.

"What's the price range?" asked Lieberman.

Bess gave him a tolerant look, the look of one who knew there were to be more of such questions to come.

"Whole package?" asked Rose.

Lieberman nodded.

"Including postage it can, for 150 invitations, range from $375 to $550 or a little more."

"For invitation cards?"

"That's a 20 percent discount figure," said Esther. "The stamps are usually thirty-seven cents to send and thirty-seven cents for the return envelope."

"I like the one on page twenty-seven," Bess said.

Esther expertly opened the album to page twenty-seven. Lieberman leaned forward to look. It was simple, ivory colored with a blue border and blue invitation lettering.

"Barry?" Lieberman asked.

"It's fine," Barry said, squirming.

"Settled," said Rose with a smile.

"Awkward as the question might be," said Lieberman, "how much will that one cost?"

"That's in category A-14," said Rose. "Three hundred and eighty, that's with the 20 percent already taken off, the response cards and thank-you notes included."

Bess gave her husband a look that told him life would be easier for him if he backed off.

"Category A-14 it shall be," said Lieberman.

But it was only beginning.

The yarmulkes with Barry's name and the date. The color and quality of the little caps that men wore to the service and were taken home as tokens of remembrance. Bess, who would have been enjoying this were it not for her husband's thoughts of their savings and her grandson's desire to escape, selected blue yarmulkes. Barry and Abe looked at each other and agreed. One hundred and eighty dollars.

Lieberman was being led into what he knew the big-ticket items were going to be.

By the time it was over, he had been cajoled, intimidated, and worked over before finally agreeing to: (a) a Kiddush, refreshments after the Friday night service for the congregation and guests, at a cost of $900, (b) an Oneg Shabbat in the temple dining room for all following the Saturday morning services, such lunch to include a buffet of herring in sour cream, tuna salad, egg salad, bagels, cream cheese, nova lox, a green salad, dessert table, coffee, punch, and a hot pasta dish for the kids who wouldn't eat anything else,(c) a small dinner for out-of-town guests on Friday night, (d) a small Saturday night dinner for family and friends in the Lieberman house. All of the preceding to be kosher-catered by Carl Zimmer, a member of the congregation who owned a successful catering service.

Total cost for the preceding: $4,500, a bargain.

It could have been worse. Most of the bar and bat mitzvah kids had big Saturday night parties at a hotel where a loud DJ kept them dancing, and adults tried to carry on conversations to no avail. There was nothing Jewish about such celebrations, and it would have doubled the cost. The house needed a new roof. Savings could go quickly for this event, and in the back of both Abe and Bess's minds was that in shortly less than four years they would be going through it again with Melisa.

Instead of the big party, however, Barry readily agreed to a trip to New York for five days. On each day, in addition to normal New York excursions to the Central Park Zoo, the Museum of Natural History, Broadway shows, and the Statue of Liberty, they would do one Jewish thing every day. The Yiddish Theater, Ellis Island, the Jewish Museum, a Shabbat with Bess's ultra-Orthodox cousin in Brooklyn. They could fly Southwest, stay with relatives. Melisa would stay with her father and stepmother, which was fine with her. She fully expected to have five days of being spoiled.

When the Pinchuk sisters had silently packed up their caravan, shook hands with Lieberman, exchanged hugs with Bess, and smiled at Barry, they were ushered to the door, where they carried on their perpetual argument about who was to drive their shared automobile back home. Rose reminded Esther that Esther had driven to the Liebermans and, therefore, it was Rose's turn.

The last thing the Liebermans heard as they closed the front door was Esther saying, "But I see better at night."

When they turned away from the closed door, Barry was gone, fled to the sanctuary of his bedroom upstairs. The house was old, small. There were two small bedrooms upstairs and Abe and Bess's bedroom downstairs.

"How was I?" asked Lieberman.

Bess touched his cheek.

"Better than I expected."

"I'm resigned," said Abe, moving back to the dining room. "I'm resigned. I'm tired. I'm hungry. I want to know what you've been doing all day, and I don't want to talk about what I've been doing."

"Kitchen," Bess said, leading the way.

Lieberman followed. There was something in the way she had said 'kitchen' that made him wary. There was an I've-got-something-to-tell-you in that single word. There was further evidence at the small kitchen table with the white Formica top. A place was set for one, and Lieberman could smell forbidden food as Bess pressed the preset button on the microwave on the counter next to the sink.

"Brisket," he said.

He sat, and his wife nodded as she moved to the refrigerator to get a bottle of California wine, red wine. Normally, Lieberman drank only at the Sabbath dinner, and then only a single glass.

"You have a 'topic,'" he said, as the bell went off in the microwave.

She nodded again, removed the plate of brisket and mashed potatoes from the microwave, and poured him a glass of wine, not in the everyday tumblers they had used for more than a decade but in a wineglass. Lieberman liked the feel of a fragile wineglass as much or more than he enjoyed the wine itself.

"Eat," Bess said, sitting next to him in the small kitchen.

The brisket smelled perfect. The mound of smashed potatoes, potatoes mashed without removing the skins, looked perfect and smelled of garlic. In front of his plate was the butter dish. To actually serve him butter meant that the "topic" was serious indeed.

He ate a piece of brisket and put a small slice of butter on his potatoes before he said, "The roof."

"The roof," Bess repeated.

"You've got the estimates," he said, trying the potatoes. They were perfect. He took a sip of wine.

"All three," she said. "It's an old house. An old roof."

"The roof of this house is younger than I am," he said. "In Europe houses last for hundreds of years without needing new roofs. Why is that?"

"I don't know. What I do know is that our roof leaks, Abe. We've got to have a new roof before winter."

"We just committed our savings to a bar mitzvah," he said.

"Not everything," she said. "We can get a home improvement loan for the roof. I talked to Irv Greenblatt at the bank."

"Loans have to be paid back," Lieberman said, finding that the direction of the conversation was not curbing his appetite as he had expected. "They're funny that way."

"Monthly payments," she said.

"We haven't finished paying off the car."

"You're telling me something I don't know? Abe, the roof will cave in when we get a heavy snow."

"I'll talk to God about speeding up global warming."

"You and I will talk to Irv Greenblatt about signing for a loan for $14,000."

Lieberman stopped chewing on a particularly delicious and slightly fatty piece of meat. He met his wife's eyes.

"That's not much less than we paid for this house," he said.

"We've lived here for almost thirty-five years, Abe."

"Let's sell the house," he said. "That woman who came by last year from the real estate company. We've got her card somewhere. She said we could get at least $135,000 for the house, and we don't owe a dime on it."

"You can't sell a house with a bad roof," Bess said patiently. "And we'd have to replace the carpets before anyone would buy it. Where would we get the money for that?

And where would we move? We've got the kids."

Abe ate silently for a few minutes.

"Remember Stan Taradash?" he asked.

Bess was accustomed to her husband's abrupt transitions, and tonight she was inclined to humor him.

"I remember," she said.

"High school, class clown, gangly. All arms and legs. Glasses. Dumb grin. Couldn't play basketball, baseball. Didn't even get great grades. Always had his hand up to answer questions. Shot it up in the air pumping toward the ceiling."

Lieberman demonstrated.

"He was in your class, Abe. I was six years behind."

"But you knew him."

"Everyone in Marshall High School knew him."

"Now."

"Now he's retired. Made millions in real estate. Owns a dozen office buildings in the loop. Housing developments in Northbrook, Highland Park, Park Forest. Gets his picture in the paper. Always looks serious. You have a point here, Abe?"

Lieberman looked at the food before him.

"I'm a sixty-year-old policeman, a sergeant," he said.

"Tell me something I don't know," said Bess patiently.

"You know why I've never been promoted?"

"Of course," she said. "Are we going to go over it again? If we are, I need a glass of wine."

"I'll give the short version. I have no talent for leadership. It's not in me. Wasn't in my father. Not in my brother. No talent for it. No interest in it. Consequently . . ."

Bess did pour herself a glass of wine.

"You don't make as much money as a garbageman, a teacher, as Stan Taradash."

"But I have the same expenses," he said, pointing his fork for emphasis.

"So, you'll retire in a few years, and you can be a security consultant like you've said. A Jewish detective, remember? You can line up clients, get rich in your golden years."

"When do we sign the papers? For the loan?"

"Tomorrow afternoon or morning. You stop by the bank when you can. I'll sign on my own."

"One more question," he said.

"Ask."

"What's for dessert?"

It was at that point 9:52 P.M. The phone rang. Bess got it, said hello, listened for a moment, then handed it to Abe, who had almost finished his food. The voice on the other end was Nestor Briggs, who was on the desk at the Clark Street Station. Nestor told him about the two dead men floating off the beach at Morse Avenue, told him that both corpses had been identified and that Lieberman might be particularly interested in one of them. When Nestor gave him the name of the dead man, Lieberman asked him to call Bill Hanrahan.

"Trying to find him now," said Nestor. "Not at home. His cell phone's off."

"Try the Black Moon."

"Will do," said Nestor calmly.

"How's Panther?" asked Lieberman, wiping his mouth with the napkin he had taken from his lap.

Panther was Nestor's dog, a placid, small mongrel whom Nestor occasionally brought to the station at night. Nestor lived alone with the dog. When the dog came to the station he sat quietly behind the reception desk, a bowl of water and a bowl of food in front of him. Panther simply sat, tongue out, panting, watching Nestor, who from time to time reached down to pat him gently on the head or back.

"Needs his teeth looked at," said Nestor. "But otherwise fine."

"Black Moon," Lieberman repeated, and moved to the wall to hang up the phone.

"Floaters," said Lieberman, turning to his wife.

Bess had been around policemen long enough to know what he meant and know that there was a reason he had been called. She would go to bed early, read, fall asleep after watching *Nightline*, and wake up whenever he came home. It was what she did. It was what he did.

When he did come home, he would remove his gun and holster, put them in the drawer next to his side of the bed, lock the drawer with the key he wore around his neck, kiss her gently, and tell her to go back to sleep.

Lieberman was an insomniac, which, along with heredity, accounted for his tired-hound-dog face. While he slept little, he spent a great deal of time watching very old movies on television and reading in the bathtub.

"Yes to the Pinchuk girls," he said. "Yes to the roof. Any other concessions to be made to pave the road to our eventual impoverishment?"

"Not at the moment," she said with a smile. "Be careful."

It was what she always said.

He would check the refrigerator when he got home for the dessert. He was sure it would be something special.

4

Bill Hanrahan had a favorite booth at the Black Moon Chinese Restaurant at the Lakefront Inn. The motel was located on North Lake Shore Drive a few blocks down from Devon. If you stepped out on the sidewalk during the day, you could look north and see the south end of Loyola University where Sheridan Road curved. If you looked across the street, you could see the Michigan Towers, the high-rise condo building, and you could hear the lapping of waves on the beach beyond the tall condos if the traffic was light.

Hanrahan's favorite booth was in the rear of the small restaurant near the kitchen. He sat with his back to the window. He did not like to look at the Michigan Towers. It was in the Black Moon three years earlier that he had sat at a table by the window watching the front of the condo. His job had been to watch the entrance, protect a hooker informant who lived in the building.

The hooker had been murdered while he sat in the Black Moon that night. There was a good chance she would have lived had Hanrahan been sober.

He had sat there watching the entrance across the street,

a lapsed Catholic, a former football player with a pair of bad knees, a fifty-year-old cop whose wife of twenty-five years had left him and one of whose two sons wanted nothing to do with him.

On the night Estralda Valdez had been murdered, Detective William Hanrahan had hit bottom and had little interest in climbing up. But on the night Estralda Valdez had been murdered, Bill Hanrahan had begun his rebirth . . . and it was all due to the waitress who served him chicken lo mien, Iris Chen, whose father owned the Black Moon.

And now he sat across from Iris in the booth, dead sober, as he had been for almost three years, planning their wedding. Iris was clearly beautiful. Two years older than Hanrahan, who was about to celebrate his fifty-third birthday, she looked twenty years younger. Iris was svelte. Yes, it was a word Hanrahan would not have used, but Abe had described her that way once, and it fit. They looked a bit odd together, the bulky, clearly Irish cop with the ruddy face and the svelte Chinese beauty, but they also seemed somehow right together.

Iris looked nothing like his first wife Maureen, who had, with good reason, left him and moved out of the state. Maureen was tall, pale, with a sweeping head of wavy traditional red hair, a way of shaking her head no when her husband was drinking or even thinking about drinking, or when he had done something that hinted at the suicidal when he was on the job. Maureen had counted on Lieberman to keep his partner from self-destruction, but eventually Hanrahan's self-destruction was no longer the point. It was her own survival that had been at stake, and she had left him one day and Bill had understood.

"You're sure?" he asked Iris.

She nodded. The decision was much harder for her than for him. Iris's father, who was still in the kitchen, was less than enthusiastic about the marriage. Iris's family was clearly less than joyful and, perhaps most important, a certain elderly and highly respected Chinese criminal of great reputation and power in the Chinese community was particularly displeased. It had been Laio Woo's plan to marry Iris himself. It was not sex that drove him to his desire for her. He was beyond that. She was a lady, a lady in a traditional Chinese sense. She would complete his sense of worth, sitting by his side, serving tea, being respected. For respect was what this former Shanghai street gang member sought most. He prized his antiques, conducted his illegal activities at a distance, surrounded himself with able, well-dressed young men who were both educated and completely loyal sociopaths.

Iris had been promised to this man. Iris had met Bill Hanrahan. Hanrahan, with Lieberman's help, had faced the modern-day war lord. The result had been a reluctantly granted victory for Hanrahan and Iris, an agreement to wait a full year before marrying to be sure that they both wished this, to recognize what this decision would mean to her family, her honor, her future.

"I'm sure," Iris said, reaching over to touch his hand on the table.

A paper napkin with the Chinese astrological signs lay before him with his plate, a half-finished egg roll and cup of coffee resting on it.

They had decided not to wait the full year. They had decided just a few moments earlier to get married in two days.

•

Part of the reason was that they had remained chastely apart through their entire strange courtship with one exception.

Part of the reason was that Hanrahan felt his Irish father in him, his father who had also been a cop, his father who would have gotten the Chinese gangster alone somehow and made his head ring like a gong with his nightstick.

Hanrahan had, to some degree, returned to the church with the help of a priest, had fully returned to sobriety with the help of AA, and had certainly returned to life with the help of Iris Chen.

"Then let's do it," he said. "Two days from today. Thursday."

They couldn't get married in a Catholic church. Hanrahan was divorced. Iris was a Buddhist. It was Father Sam Parker at St. Bart's who had suggested the Unitarian minister in Evanston. The former Catholic priest at the Unitarian church had readily agreed and waited only for the date.

"Two days from today?" she asked, looking around at the only two customers in the restaurant, an older couple at a table near the window who tried not to eavesdrop on their conversation. "There is so much to prepare. I want to invite my friends, my sisters, my cousins, my family."

"Will they come?" he asked.

"I think so," she said. "Don't you want people there?"

"Abe and Bess," he said. "My son Michael. He'll come. Maybe some of the people I work with. Kearney."

"My father would like to give a wedding party."

"Your father would not like to give a wedding party. Your father would like me to disappear."

"He is learning to like you," Iris said.

"Tolerate," said Hanrahan. "I'm a white, divorced, Irish Catholic cop fighting a steep battle with the bottle. And your father's got Laio Woo on his back."

Iris's father had been opposed to the wedding, afraid of his daughter getting involved with this hulking Irish policeman, afraid of the wrath of Woo the elderly gang lord, afraid of the reaction from his own family and friends. But over the past year he had begun to adjust to his daughter's determination.

"I'll ask my father to have a party on the weekend," Iris said. "I'll invite my friends and family to that. We can keep the church wedding small."

"Sounds fine," said Hanrahan with a smile. "The party'll be here?"

"No," she said. "My father will find a place. Nothing big, but I want it to be special. I have never been married before, and I will never be married again. I may not be a young girl, but I am a woman, and I want memories. I know we won't have children. You want none, and I am beyond the age of bearing."

"We've talked about this," he said.

"William," she said. "Would you consider something for me?"

"I'll consider anything for you."

"Would you consider adopting a child, a girl?"

"A baby?"

"No, a young girl. She is six. Her mother and father are dead. She is in Taiwan. Her father was white. She is the child of an old friend."

"Adopt a child," he said to himself. "Iris, I'm a rotten father."

"You were not a good father," she said. "But you could be one *now*."

"A girl," he said. "I have two grown boys, grandchildren."

"Consider it," she said. "For me. For us."

Hanrahan was considering what to think, what to say, when he heard the phone ring on the glass counter against the back wall. Iris got up and moved to the phone.

Hanrahan looked at the red dragons and black moons that decorated the walls.

"For you," Iris called.

Hanrahan got up and went to the phone.

"Hanrahan," he said.

"Nestor. Meet Abe at the Morse Avenue Beach. Two floaters."

"Why us?" Hanrahan asked.

"There's a reason, William. You'll see. Since you're at the Black Moon, how about picking up a couple of egg rolls for Panther?"

"What . . ."

Briggs had hung up. Morse Avenue Beach was no more than ten minutes away from the Black Moon. He looked at Iris, reached over, and took her hand.

"Lot to think about," he said. "I've got to work. Can you give me a couple of egg rolls?"

Iris returned the touch and would have kissed him had the couple not been sitting at the window.

"She's a very pretty child," Iris said.

As he headed for the door after Iris had gotten the egg rolls from the kitchen and handed them to Hanrahan in a small, brown paper bag, Hanrahan found himself giving serious consideration to the completely alien idea of becoming a father again. It didn't feel nearly as strange or unpleasant as he thought it should.

Wychovski was cold. Wychovski was wet. Wychovski couldn't get the words to songs out of his head as he crossed a street heading west, away from the water. He had forty dollars in wet bills in his wallet. About eighty cents in change. There was money, not a hell of a lot, in a bank in St. Louis, if he could get to the bank in St. Louis, if the cops had not already identified him, if he could get out of town, if, if, if, if. It was all Pryor's fault. Well not all, but enough.

" 'What do you do in a case like that,' " he sang softly, teeth chattering. " 'What do you do but jump on your hat, and your grandmother and your toothbrush and anything that's helpless.' "

Where did those lines come from? Where had he heard that song? When he was a kid. That was it. He had a record when he was a kid. Who sang that song? Gibson something.

It was a residential street at least six blocks from the water. He wasn't sure if he was in Evanston or Chicago. Probably Evanston. He could jack a car, be gone in seconds, but someone might see him. It wasn't late enough or dark enough, and walking, at least for a while, would be safer. Maybe.

He headed south. Somehow he felt he could hide more easily in Chicago. Weighted down with golden animals and, he hoped, waterproof watches. He needed clothes or a place to dry out. He needed to find a bus or an el train. He couldn't take a chance on a cab. Cabby might remember him. Cops might ask cabbies. Cops were funny that way when a cop was killed. Not that they wouldn't care about the dead jeweler, but a dead cop was special.

He tried to walk slowly, glancing at the few cars that came up or down the street. If he spotted a cop car, he would slowly walk up the nearest driveway, take his keys out of his pocket, and pretend to be moving toward the door. If that failed to keep the cop car going, he would have run like hell, which, given his wet clothes and soggy socks and shoes, would have been difficult.

Wychovski had stayed in reasonably good condition behind the walls. He had taken up jogging and running, and lifting, more to keep away from the general prison population than for a love of the exercise; but he had gotten used to it and knew he had the endurance if not the speed for a long foot chase. He looked like a small bull. He wanted to look at least like a dapper bull and not a damp one.

No cop cars. Few people.

"There is no trick to the cancan. It is so easy to do."

Another song. He could hear a gravelly voice singing inside him. Bobby Short. That was the name. No trick to the cancan. Maybe Wychovski should cancan his way down the street. Maybe the day and night had made him a little crazy. Maybe he should come up with some plan.

Wychovski walked three blocks, passing only a couple of black kids in their teens wearing shorts. They hardly looked at him. Even if they had mugging on their minds, the wet guy walking past them looked like a compact car with a bad attitude. They were busy dribbling and singsong talking. "I could'a taken his ass to the paint any goddamn fuckin' time I wanted to. Know what I mean? But that fuckin' Stoner, man. He don't know how to set a pick or get out of the way. He just stands out there blocking the lane. Know what I mean? Wants the ball. Wants the ball."

Wants the ball, Wychovski thought. Everybody wants the ball. Now I've got the ball. Pryor is dead. Crazy Pryor. Stupid Pryor. Now I'm walking who knows where with no plan.

He came to a street, a wider street than the one he had been walking. More cars. To his left, he thought, he could see the lake, wondered if he wandered over he might see Pryor's body floating past. Maybe he would wave good-bye to him or give him the finger.

Distracted. There was an old iron fence across the street. No longer protected by the apartment buildings and houses, he felt a chill breeze off the lake and shuddered at the headstones beyond the fence. The fence extended in both directions. The iron spikes were old at the top but still pointed. He was in reasonable condition, but he was tired and wet. Chances were fair that he might slip and get skewered trying to go over it. Besides, what would he do in a cemetery? Hide? He was too cold to hide in a cemetery.

The dead didn't bother him. Almost everyone was dead, he thought as he walked to his right a little faster than he had before because there were more cars on the street. Eventually one had to be a cop.

What happened to all the dead? Thousands of years and we're not surrounded by cemeteries and up to our asses in dead bodies. Layers beneath there were probably bones from Indians a thousand, two thousand years ago. He was walking on dead dinosaurs and people. Everyone in the world was.

He passed the cemetery and in another block came to

an even bigger street. The sign said it was Chicago. Was that just the name of the street or was he in Chicago? He turned left, knowing that was where the city was. Maybe he could cross the line somewhere, be out of the jurisdiction of the Evanston cops. He didn't know how it worked.

Across the street running to and from Chicago was an embankment. At the top of it were elevated train tracks. Good. He would walk till he came to a station. He kept walking. Lots of cars coming and going now. No houses. Small businesses, closed for the night.

Think. I can't. Think. Okay. Clothes. No time. No luck. He came to another intersection with an even busier street, which the sign told him was Howard. Vaguely, he remembered or thought he remembered or just wanted to remember that Howard was the dividing line between Chicago and Evanston.

He was standing in front of a flower shop on the corner. It was closed. Across the street was an old storefront building with closed shops downstairs and a darkened beauty school upstairs, its windows shouting that haircuts were five dollars at the Hair Artists School of Beauty. "Stop in. Save." That was in one of the dark windows.

He had lost the train tracks, which had veered to the left. He moved left. Think of a reason why you're wet. Fell in the lake. Kids for no reason came out of the dark with buckets and doused him. The kids laughed and taunted. They pointed their fingers at him. Their teeth were large. They were black. They wore shorts. One of them had a basketball. They bounced the basketball off of his head. He should have gone to the police, but he didn't want trouble. He was from out of town.

Did that make sense? Maybe. It was weird enough.

Weird sometimes made more sense than falling in the lake.

All the faces of the people on the street were black. He got glances but no comments, no hassles. He was tired, but he wouldn't take any hassles. He might even, in some strange way, welcome it. He was stronger than he looked.

No one better mess with him. He shouldn't have run when those kids soaked him and hit him with a basketball. Wait. That didn't happen. Hell, from now on it is what happened.

A break, or maybe. A store across the street was open, one of those stores with the big sign that says everything is a dollar but when you get in some things are two or three dollars, but what the hell.

An elevated train rattled less than half a block away. He crossed the street in the middle of the block, dodging a red car with a dented radiator.

The Big Dollar store. A black woman behind the counter. Two other black women talking to her on the other side of the counter. They weren't talking English. It sounded something like French. The woman behind the counter was young, dark, kind of pretty. The other two women were older, heavier.

They looked at him.

"Fireplug burst over on Chicago Street when I walked past it," he said. "Need some dry clothes till I get home."

The pretty woman nodded and went back to her conversation. The prices were up to five dollars, but he managed a pair of cheap blue pants made out of everything synthetic in China, a pullover blue short-sleeved polo shirt with the letter "P" in white on the pocket, three pairs of white underwear, a pair of white socks, some made-in-Indonesia cloth sneakers with plastic soles that would hold up for no more than a month, and a gray long-sleeved sweatshirt with pockets and a hood. Total bill: twenty-three-dollars. Wychovski was a five-hundred-dollar suit man for chrissake. Prison gray or Big Dollar clothes. He would settle for nothing in between. But that was then. This is now.

He handed a twenty and a five to the talking woman, who looked just as pretty close up. The other two women kept talking.

"Anyplace I can change?" he said as affably as he could.

"Rest room in the back," she said. "You need a key."

She had a nice accent. The key was attached to a big round piece of orange plastic that announced in blue letters UNIVERSITY OF ILLINOIS.

Things were looking up, Wychovski decided as he changed. Not far up. Not high. Not yet. As he changed he made his decision. These were desperate times. Desperate times called for desperate measures. Who had said that? George Washington? Thomas Paine? Wychovski had read so goddamn much in prison he couldn't remember who had written what.

Plan: Get on the train. Get off in three or four stops. Jack a car and find Walter the fence. Walter would have to buy the gold pieces in his pocket. If he didn't, Wychovski had no choice. He'd take the fence. Walter touched the Glock wedged now inside the pocket of his hooded gray sweatshirt. It was bad business robbing fences. Walter would be protected.

But desperate times. Desperate measures.

The bodies were lying under the white beach lights on the dark sand. The nearest light about twenty feet over their heads was sputtering, giving notice that it had had enough of graffiti-covered rocks and benches, fornicating teens, and the dumped remnants of drug users who liked to shoot, snort, and smoke to the sound of waves and the smell of dead fish.

"Looks like God and Moses," said Hanrahan, standing next to his partner.

"I think it's God and Adam," Lieberman answered, hands in his pockets, watching the uniformed cops marking off the crime scene or what regulations said was the crime scene until otherwise informed.

"The Sistine Chapel," said Hanrahan.

"I've seen pictures. Never been to Europe."

"Me either."

They both knew this about each other but it was something to say while they watched and waited. A night breeze swept in. For an instant Hanrahan thought he had something in his eye. He wiped it with his thumb. It was nothing.

It was not the first time a floater had come to a temporary stop off the beach next to the granite breaker. It was a bus stop on the way to nowhere in particular depending on the wind, the tide, and the weather. The lake pushed them against the breaker for an hour or so, then sent them on their way. The lakefront along the beach was a regular patrol stop, mostly to drive out druggies, discourage muggers, and look for the occasional body. This, however, was the first time either detective could remember two bodies turning up here at the same time.

The bodies had been pulled from the surf by the uniformed cops. Both cops had worn boots they kept in the back of their patrol car. These cops weren't kids. They knew boots were essential for surf, alleys, Dumpsters, and whatever else the human and animal world could create that smelled foul and wet and dead.

The two bodies were men. There was somewhat of a resemblance to Michelangelo's painting. The fingers of the two men, one over the other, were almost touching, but the two men looked neither biblical nor noble.

Both were dressed, one in a gray sweatshirt, the other in slacks, white shirt open at the neck, with sports jacket spread like limp wings, no tie. Both were soaked. The dead man in the sweatshirt had thin hair covering his face, pasted down. His eyes were closed. The other man's eyes and mouth were open.

One of the uniformed cops came over to the detectives, careful to avoid the marked-off area. The cop was no more than forty but carrying a beer gut and no expression.

His name was Genfredo. Bill and Abe knew him.

"ID on both," Genfredo said. "Wallets. Littler guy had eighty-seven dollars. Bigger one had seventeen."

"We know the bigger one," said Lieberman. "Who's the smaller one?"

"Name's Pryor, Matthew Alvin Pryor. Shot full of holes. Call came a few hours ago. I think he took the bullets from the Skokie police. Jewelry story robbery. Had a partner. Partner's missing. Got a description. Matthew Alvin went in the water off the rocks in Evanston after a chase. He or his partner killed a jewelry store owner in Northbrook and a cop in Skokie."

"They got around," said Hanrahan.

"They got around," Genfredo said, looking at the bodies. "The other guy hasn't been in the water as long."

"That one we know," said Hanrahan. "Name's Sokol. We saw him on a charge early in the morning. Looks like he didn't even have a chance to change clothes."

"That why they called you two?" asked Genfredo, looking back at his partner, who was going along the water's edge with a flashlight.

"I made a report," said Abe. "Copy to Kearney, copy to Evanston police. Computer did the link. Here we stand."

Alan Kearney was a lieutenant at the Clark Street Station, a handsome, tormented-looking man who had made a mistake a few years earlier that would keep him a lieutenant till he quit or retired or walked away.

"Shall we?" asked Lieberman.

Hanrahan nodded, and the three men walked over to the bodies, both of which had been laid out on their backs.

"When Davidson took the last one," Genfredo said, "he

bitched because we pulled it in. I told him the lake was about to take the corpse back out. It was that or maybe lose him. Davidson didn't give a shit."

"He's got hemorrhoids," said Hanrahan.

"Shitting on me won't cure 'em," said Genfredo. "I'm glad it was your call."

"We're ecstatic," said Lieberman dryly, looking down at what remained of Arnold Sokol, which was actually quite a lot considering that the back of his head was crushed, a sharded skull open to reveal darkness and the hint of darkening brain matter. Sokol's shirt was open, and the detectives could clearly see the seven or eight dark deep bruises on his chest and stomach. One of Arnold Sokol's eyes was a dark empty hole. Fish or foul play. Too soon to tell.

Hanrahan looked back down the street at the ambulance with flashing lights but no siren heading their way. It was late. Both men in the Michelangelo pose were definitely dead. No need to give the alarm like an ice-cream truck that would bring out gawkers, beach clutterers, and the living dead.

"Poor schmuck," said Lieberman, looking down at Sokol.

"Amen," said Hanrahan.

There really wasn't more to say unless the young cop combing the beach with a flashlight came up with a weapon or something interesting that might relate to the two dead men. It wasn't likely. It didn't happen. It was up to the medical examiner.

"How do we call it?" asked Hanrahan.

It was a tricky pair of corpses. Neither had probably died in Chicago on or near the beach in East Rogers Park. But they had landed here, and the pair was theirs, though they would check in with the cops in Skokie, Evanston, and Northbrook. The Skokie cops would be interested because Pryor or his partner had killed one of theirs. The Northbrook cops would be interested because Pryor or his partner had killed a citizen. The Evanston cops would be interested because they had put the bullets in Pryor and their township had an incident report that involved Sokol.

The ambulance came to a stop as close to the beach as it could get. Two paramedics jumped out, leaving the lights on and the blue-and-white ball rotating. There was no point in telling them to slow down. The paramedics had already been informed that the men were dead, but there was procedure to follow, and who knew what might happen, so they followed the book and come running.

Both were young. Both had mustaches. Both were big.

"A pair," said the first, moving toward Pryor.

"Not a matched pair," said Lieberman. "They met by chance."

The paramedics used their eyes and stethoscopes and came to the conclusion that both men, one full of bullets, the other covered with what appeared to be knife wounds, were really most sincerely dead.

"We take 'em?" asked one of the medics, rising.

"Be our guest," said Lieberman.

There was no need to tell them to move quickly. They had other stops to make and a long night ahead. Lieberman and Hanrahan watched as the bodies were zipped into black bags and carried away. They checked the indentations in the sand where the bodies had been and saw nothing besides cigarette butts and a Zagnut candy wrapper.

The ambulance left as quietly as it had come.

"Anything?" Genfredo called to his partner, who stood in one place scanning the shore with his flashlight.

"Nothing you'd want me to show you," the younger cop said. "Unless you're in the mood for a very large, very dead, very black Coho salmon."

The cop with the gut didn't bother to answer.

"Take down the tape," said Lieberman. "Write it up. Bring it in when you come off duty."

"You got it," said Genfredo, waving to his partner.

Hanrahan and Lieberman moved back to the street. Cars were parked illegally all along the turnaround. The neighborhood was an overnight parking nightmare. Apartment buildings four, five, seven stories high. Narrow passageways between. Not enough garages in the alleys to take in a tenth of those who lived in the neighborhood, signs all over the place telling them they couldn't park here, there, wherever. Every few weeks, cops like Genfredo and his partner would spend their shift, providing there were no floaters, muggers, or Vietnamese husbands who went berserk and hacked up their families, giving out parking tickets that helped pay their salaries.

"Station?" asked Hanrahan.

Lieberman shrugged. Not much choice. They had people to call, a suspect to find, a widow to inform, coffee to drink, another report to write while they waited for a medical examiner's report.

"How's Iris, Father Murph?" Lieberman asked.

"Holding up, Rabbi," said Hanrahan. "We're going ahead. Still up for best man?"

"I'll bring a glass for you to step on," said Lieberman.

"Would Thursday suit you?"

"This Thursday?"

"Unitarian church in Evanston. Six o'clock. You and Bess still willing to stand up for us?"

"We'll be there," said Lieberman.

"You're walking funny, Rabbi."

"Hit my hip in Zembinsky's hospital room. I'll be alright."

"Hungry?"

"When am I not?"

"Stop at Park's on Devon?"

"I'm on the way."

They stopped at a Korean shop, which called itself a deli, picked up some sandwiches, and headed for the Clark Street Station.

Nestor was on the desk. He looked up at them over the top of his glasses. He liked the effect on perps and angry victims. Nestor thought he looked a little like the actor M. Emmett Walsh. He was right. Hanrahan tossed him the brown paper bag of egg rolls.

There was no one in the small lobby. Nestor nodded thanks as they walked past and up the stairs to the squad room. That wasn't empty, but it wasn't full either. It was a Tuesday. Tuesdays were slow. No one knew why. A professor at the University of Chicago had written an article on crime patterns in the city, which days were more likely to be busy, which were more likely to be light. He had had a pair of assistants given to him on a grant doing research going back to the days of Johnny Torio.

There had been a lot of bad Tuesdays, but statistically they were definitely, over the course of eighty years or more, significantly lighter than other days. And those bad Tuesdays had been on nights when there was a full moon. Like tonight. The professor had forwarded some theories

about why all this might be so. None of them had made
sense to Lieberman, and none of them had made any difference. You worked your shift or were called in or stayed
over if you were on a roll. No day was a vacation. One of
his worst days had been a Tuesday when five uniformed
cops on Montrose were gunned down by a gang of Irish
kids called the Rocks. The Rocks, short for Shamrocks,
were angry because their leader had been pulled in for a
murder. Leaderless, they had gone to their number two, a
sixteen-year-old kid named Dickey, whose answer to almost
everything was "Let's kill the fuckin' bastards."

That had been a Tuesday. They had started at about six,
and by midnight they had rounded up the Rocks—all except Dickey, who had seen too many IRA movies and went
down in a blaze of nothing that resembled glory.

When they were seated at Lieberman's desk near the
window, sandwiches and coffee in front of them, Lieberman said, "Let's see if Zembinsky is still comfortably con-
templating his young life of crime in Evanston Hospital."

He was, but they both remembered that there had been
a phone in the room. Lieberman made a note to check any
calls Zembinsky had made.

Hanrahan went through Sokol's wet wallet, found his
driver's license and his address.

"Chicago," said Hanrahan. "Sheridan Road, north of
Devon. Washed up a few blocks from home. Nice address.
We split up. You want the widow or the kid in the hospi-
tal?"

"Neither," said Lieberman. "Who played the lecher in
Mildred Pierce?"

"Easy," said Hanrahan, "Zachary Scott. Unless you
mean Jack Carson."

"How the hell did you know that?"

"You asked me that one before, Rabbi. You're getting old."

"I was born old. You take the widow? I'll take the hospital?"

The kid in the hospital was, at least by birth if not by choice, a Jew. The widow was Catholic. It might make no difference who took which lead, but there might be some slight touch, some contact.

The kid wasn't going to be easy, but it was a hell of a lot better than telling a woman her husband had been murdered unless she had killed him, which was always possible, almost anything was possible.

They ate slowly. Abe a tuna on white. Bill a turkey on rye with mayo and onions. Coffee. It was almost midnight.

"What about the other one?" Hanrahan asked.

"Cop killer? Let's find out who Pryor is. Maybe that leads us to the man that got away."

"It's a start. Abe?"

"I know."

"We should talk to the other widow. The one in Northbrook, the jewelry store. I'll check with the Northbrook cops, see if she can give us a description of Pryor's buddy."

"It's nights like this that make being a cop worthwhile," said Lieberman dryly.

Hanrahan looked at his partner. There was no telling if Abe was tired. He always looked the same—weary, baggy-eyed.

"How's the bar mitzvah coming?" asked Hanrahan.

"I may have to sell my boat," said Lieberman.

"You haven't got a boat."

"Then I'll sell my shares in Microsoft."

"You've got shares in Microsoft?"

"No, you?"

"No shares in anything."

Lieberman sat silently, cheeks full of sandwich. He needed a Tylenol for his hip pain.

"We're gonna keep the wedding . . ."

"Cheap?"

"Inexpensive."

"Maybe I can get Barry married instead of bar mitzvahed," said Lieberman.

"It'd be cheaper," said Hanrahan. "If you let the Unitarians handle it."

"Know any nice Jewish girls between eleven and twenty?"

"No," said Hanrahan. "Wait. Yes, your granddaughter."

"You are not being helpful, Father Murph."

Hanrahan finished the last of his sandwich.

"Sorry, Rabbi. Will you settle for a Chinese girl? Iris has a niece."

"How old?"

"Thirty-six."

"Sounds perfect," said Lieberman. "Let's discuss this further."

"Shouldn't we check with Barry?"

"I'm the patriarch," said Lieberman. "I make the decisions."

"And?"

"I'm going to empty my savings account and have a hell of a bar mitzvah, to which you are not only invited but expected to bring a substantial present I can pawn or sell to Fat Dewey to help defray the expenses."

"I'm not a wealthy man, Rabbi."

"Sell your house," said Lieberman, wiping his hands on a paper napkin. "It's for a worthy cause."

"I'm heading for the widow."

"I'm heading for the hospital. Maish's at ten in the morning?" asked Lieberman.

"Something comes up we call."

Maybe they would find time for a few hours' sleep. Maybe.

Lieberman reached down to power on his cell phone. Hanrahan did the same.

Wychovski found the car he wanted on a street called Winthrop. It was a slightly battered Honda, a 1992, maybe older. He'd pick up another one after he visited Walter. He'd pick up another one or, if he could get enough money, he would buy one, and head for St. Louis.

He wished Pryor were still alive, so he could kill him. He drove south, trying to remember where Walter's place was. Fullerton. He remembered Fullerton. When he got there, near there, he would recognize something, remember. He did not want to call Walter again. He wanted to surprise Walter. He would try to make a deal. He had pockets full of watches and little gold animals. Wychovski fingered them with his right hand while he drove with his left. Was that a horse? A zebra? A cop was dead. A jeweler was dead. A pregnant woman stood screaming in his memory.

What was the baby's name going to be? He couldn't remember. Yeah, Jessica. She would change it now. He was sure. She would name it for her dead husband. Wychovski would find a way to send a gift for the baby, he told himself. A gift from a sympathetic person who had read about the woman's tragedy. He knew he was lying to himself. He would send no gift, but he listened to his lie, and he got lost. He ran out of Sheridan Road, turned right, went by a cemetery. He tried not to look at the cemetery but he did. Graceland Cemetery. Wasn't Elvis buried in Graceland?

Wychovski remembered his grandmother in the nursing home. He had visited her just before he went back to prison the last time. She was his only living relative, and he paid her bills, at least what the government didn't cover.

His grandmother, Sophie, had been small, frail, confused, and depressed. They had tried to find something to interest her.

"You like bingo?" the young woman in large round glasses had asked patiently, kneeling next to his grandmother.

"No," she had said.

"She loves bingo," Wychovski had answered.

"Church?" the woman said. "You're a Catholic."

"I'm not."

Wychovski drove to a street he vaguely remembered, Ashland. He turned left, kept going south.

The young woman in the nursing home had come up with a list of things that might interest his grandmother. Cooking, reading, television. All "no."

"She likes game shows," Wychovski had said.

His grandmother had answered briefly in Polish. Wychovski didn't understand Polish. He understood cash, possessions, that there was only one life and nothing more and that you lived to make yourself comfortable, to satisfy your needs and wants. There was nothing more. But there was his grandmother.

"Music?" the young woman had tried.

"She likes polkas," he had said.

"No," his grandmother had answered, looking off into a corner where there was nothing to look at but a corner.

"Wait," she said, suddenly animated. "Elvis. I love Elvis."

His grandmother had decried all popular music. She had been a Lawrence Welk junkie, a Perry Como fan, and she liked Patti Page and Ginny Simms and Dinah Shore. Elvis had been an abomination to his grandmother. He had represented all that was wrong with young people. She spat three times when his name was mentioned. Chubby Checker, Fats Domino, Bill Haley, Buddy Holly were worth one spit each. The others she couldn't identify weren't worth the hint of a spit.

"I love Elvis," his grandmother declared, looking at him with a smile.

It was then he was certain of what he had only considered. His grandmother was truly out of her mind. It wasn't Alzheimer's. The doctors had assured him. It was simply dementia. She was nearing ninety years old. It happens.

"Graceland," his grandmother had said, taking the young woman's hand.

Where had his grandmother even heard of Graceland?

"I'd like to go there," she said.

"When you're better I'll take you," Wychovski had said.

Sophie had answered in Polish. The young social worker smiled. Her name was Flaherty or Flannery or something Irish. She didn't know Polish from chop suey, which his grandmother had also loved but now hated.

His grandmother had died while Wychovski was in prison. He didn't know if the nursing home had placated her with Elvis records. He had never visited her after the Elvis incident. The sight of lolling ancient people in wheelchairs in the hall outside their rooms, the one woman who kept calling "I have to be at work at nine," the old man who looked up at him, his mouth open, following Wychovski with his eyes down the long corridor, the smell of spiceless old-people food. He never went back. Not that he could have. He was arrested three weeks after that last visit with Sophie.

Past Addison, past Belmont, where he spotted a Polish restaurant. The ghost of his grandmother inside listening to polkas and Elvis and making pierogi and cabbage rolls.

Past Diversey. Dark stores, closed for the night. Past midnight. Past caring. They, the people who ran the stores, paint stores, key shops, storefront accountants, would be up in hours doing the same thing they did every day. There's safety in doing the same thing every day. No creativity. Wychovski didn't tell anyone, but he thought of himself as a master craftsman, maybe even an artist, no two days quite the same, every job a leap into a pounding blood-pressure river. Like going onstage, he was sure. Or like stepping in front of an audience to sing, or like sitting down to write a story and not knowing what would come next.

He needed a toilet.

He stopped at a twenty-four-hour Walgreen's just past Diversey near some outcropping of concrete buildings labeled Lathrope Homes. After midnight, but there were customers, mostly black. He bought a large bottle of Tylenol Plus and a generic antacid and asked for the washroom. The pharmacist on duty, old man, heavy with not much of a neck reminded him of James Earl Jones, even his voice and the way he looked at Wychovski over his glasses.

"Emergency," Wychovski said.

The pharmacist nodded, handed him a key, and pointed the way. The toilet was clean. Wychovski examined some of the animals in his pockets. He could get them melted down, but they wouldn't be worth as much as if they remained jewelry. He sat in a daze examining a cat, a pelican, a seal, a giraffe. They felt like treasure. He was a walking Noah, and the rain was falling hard.

Pryor dead. Window shattered. Cop dead.

He shoved the animals back into the den of his pocket, washed himself, and went back into the night.

If it were done, he told himself getting back into the car after downing three Tylenol and a swallow of antacid. When it is done, then better it were done quickly.

He remembered that. Wychovski was no fool. He had read in prison. Jack London, Shakespeare, anything. When he hit Fullerton it was after one in the morning. He wasn't sure whether he should turn right or left. He turned left and started to look for something that would jolt his memory.

Dark, dark, dark, but lots of traffic. Where were people going to or coming from at this hour?

Find him. Get it over with.

There was something. There on the right. A hot dog stand. Rickety, on the corner, big painting of a hot dog with mustard and onions. Wychovski had learned to like his hot dog sandwiches with mayo or ketchup. Learned it from the blacks. The place was closed, but it resonated. He was close.

Buildings that looked like dark factories. Old brick. Dirty, tired buildings. Bump over train tracks. Yes, nearby. On the left, on the corner, a bar on the first floor of a three-story building. Budweiser sign in the window. Red, glowing. Place was open. He had stopped there for a beer once, a year ago. Anniversary celebrated today in double death and overtime.

Walter was two or three doors down from the tavern. Wychovski parked, moved his gun. He hadn't noticed. It had pinched against his hip. He got out and looked across the street. Three buildings in a row. Apartments upstairs. Storefronts downstairs.

There it was. Dark. Olshan's Antiques and Used Furniture.

Wychovski waited till there was no traffic and crossed. Someone laughed in the bar on the corner. He could hear music behind the laughter. He wondered how the people who lived with the noise liked it and if they ever complained. Probably not.

He looked in the window. An old dining room set in the window with a recliner on top of the table. The recliner looked tired and heavy. There was a dim night-light at the rear of the shop. He could see furniture piled, a mess of furniture, paintings, shapes jagged and shapes round. He knocked at the door. The glass rattled. Behind the glass was a mesh of metal. It rattled, too. Nothing. He knocked again. Louder. More rattling.

"Shake, rattle, and roll," he muttered. "You never do nothing to save a doggone soul." He shifted from one leg to the other and knocked even louder, looking over his shoulder at the street, knowing that if he saw a cop car coming he would move quickly to the bar. No answer, no cop car. He moved to the bar on the corner anyway.

He pushed open the door, expecting who knew what. What he saw was a small tavern, night dark, bartender, thin, almost bald, five customers, three at the bar arguing about something on the television set, two at a table. The two at the table, a man and a woman, were old and nursing beers. They weren't even talking. They were serious drinkers. The woman was overweight. The man was fat.

Wychovski moved to the bar. One of the old men turned to look at him.

"You settle it," the man said. His face was red, and he needed a shave. His eyes were nearly closed. "The greatest Cub of all, all time, ever."

"Banks," said one of the other old men.

"Nicholson," said another.

"And I," said the man with the nearly closed eyes, "I say Sosa hands down. Funny-looking spic's going in the record books."

Wychovski shrugged and ordered a beer. The bartender nodded and brought it.

"Well?" asked the old man.

"I'm from Texas," said Wychovski.

"Rangers," sighed the old man, turning away.

Wychovski laid a couple of bucks on the bar and asked the bartender, "Walter, the furniture store. I've got to see him."

The bartender looked at Wychovski, who didn't look like a cop but wasn't a regular either. He didn't look like he was into drugs either, but there was something about him the bartender recognized and didn't want to catch.

"Closed for the night, I guess," said the bartender, with a cough, reaching for a burning cigarette in the glass ashtray.

"It's important," said Wychovski.

"I've got nothing to do with his business," said the bartender.

"Where does he live?"

"Over the store," the bartender said.

"Does . . ." Wychovski said.

"End of questions. End of answers. I'm closing up for the night. Finish your beer. Thanks for the business."

Wychovski knew when to stop. The bartender made the rounds of his remaining patrons and told them he was closing in ten minutes. He never looked back at Wychovski, who left his drink half-finished and went back into the night. There was a door next to Walter's shop, farther east than Wychovski had gone. No name. No lights. A bell button almost invisible in the dim streetlight. Wychovski pushed. Nothing. He leaned on the bell, put his life in his thumb. He would stand there pressing all night till someone answered or the bell or all his fingers gave out.

He didn't have to wait long, not if five minutes is long. A light came on beyond the wooden door. He could see it under the door, dim but there. Then steps coming down. Slow steps, someone walking down sure and heavy. Lots of steps. Then a voice.

"Who is it?"

It wasn't Walter behind the door. It sounded like a black man.

"My name's Wychovski. I've got to see Walter."

"Come back tomorrow."

"I can't . . ."

There was the sound of voices inside. Wychovski strained to hear. He thought the second voice might be Walter's.

"Don't come back tomorrow," the man with the black voice said. "Don't come back at all."

"I'm staying till you open," Wychovski said. "I've got a good deal in my pockets and nothing to lose. If the cops find me huddled here, they'll find a stolen car across the street, too, and I'll have to explain why I have what I have in my pockets and why I'm here with it."

More talking inside.

"Five minutes," came the black voice. "Then you get the hell out of here, deal or no deal. You go headfirst or feetfirst. Choice'll be yours."

"Deal," said Wychovski.

Bolts turned, and the door opened.

Melvin Zembinsky was in his hospital room getting dressed when Lieberman entered. Melvin had his left leg in his jeans and was trying to keep his balance while putting in his right leg. He took a little hop, made the move, got the pants on, and was pulling them up when he saw Lieberman standing at the door.

Melvin's bed was the one closest to the door. A white curtain was partially drawn between his bed and the one next to it. A television mounted on a black metal plate on the wall across from bed two was playing. It was an old game show. There was no sound. Lieberman looked up at the host of the show, Bill Cullen, who had been dead at least a decade. Shot of the audience laughing. Lieberman was not a laugher. He wasn't laughing now. He stood watching the young man.

Zembinsky's facial bruises were a darker prehealing red. A bandage was wrapped around his head, covering the stitches. He ignored the detective and reached for a shirt on the bed.

Zembinsky wasn't tall, but he was well built, flat stomach, body of an athlete. He carefully pulled the black sweat-shirt over his head, keeping himself from biting his lip to keep back the pain as he eased the shirt over his bandaged head.

Lieberman folded his arms and said nothing. Zembinsky sat on the bed and began putting his shoes on. Abe had no doubt about who would speak first.

When his socks and shoes were on, the young man looked up, and said, "What?"

"You made three phone calls. Two last night. One this morning."

Zembinsky shook his head.

"One call to the home of James Franzen a little after we left you," Lieberman went on. "A second a few hours later to Franzen again and then this morning to an Edward Denenberg."

"Dean, Ed Dean," Zembinsky corrected.

"Like James Dean?" asked Lieberman.

Zembinsky laughed and shook his head again.

"James Dean? You're even fuckin' older than you look. Why didn't you ask Dean Martin? Or Dizzy Dean?"

"You know your old people history," said Lieberman.

"My grandfather's a comedian. Was a comedian. He's dead. I've got a tape of his he made at some fucking Jew resort. My grandfather wasn't funny. He spent a year dying and telling me about all the famous people he knew. Bullshit, but what the hell. Kept talking about some guy named Harry Ritz. Now you've got my life story, and I've got my pants on."

"Your father and mother, Melvin," Lieberman said.

Zembinsky looked up.

"You want my life story, you pay for it. Charge is cut-rate, rock bottom, going-out-of-business sale. You don't call me Melvin. You call me Zembinsky or Z, you get answers."

"Parents, Z," said Lieberman.

"My father was in something called SDS in college."

"Students for a Democratic Society," Lieberman said.

A shrug from Zembinsky, who stood, testing his balance.

"Except," said Zembinsky, "they weren't democratic. Most of them weren't students. And they didn't know what society was."

"And you do?" asked Lieberman.

"You a social worker or a cop? What do you want?"

"Peace of mind, but for now I'll settle for what you talked to Eddie Dean about."

"World peace," said Zembinsky. "Albanians in Macedonia. The International Space Station. My bowel movements. Jackson Pollock's later works. None of your fuckin' business."

"It's always enlightening talking to an educated man," said Lieberman.

"Yeah, it's amazing what little pieces of useless shit you can pick up in two years in a community college. So? Sokol changed his mind? He's bringing charges?"

"Hold it down," a raspy voice called from behind the curtain. "I'm watching something here."

"Crazy fart," said Zembinsky, nodding over his shoulder. "So, am I arrested? You going to read me my rights?"

"What did you talk to Eddie about?"

"I answered that," Zembinsky said, taking a step toward Lieberman, whose back was to the door. "Now I'm checking myself out of here. It smells like iodine and old men dying."

"Eddie," Lieberman repeated.

Zembinsky shook his head and looked up at the yellow-white wall with his hands on his hips. Marlon Brando had done it better in *The Wild One*.

"You think I'm going to tell you the truth about what I talked to Eddie about?"

"I'll guess," Lieberman said, as Zembinsky took another step toward him. The young man had forty years and forty pounds on the detective. Lieberman didn't move. "You talked about getting Sokol."

Zembinsky did his best to look bored. It was caricature Marlon Brando.

"Getting Sokol," Zembinsky repeated. "Getting him what?"

"Getting him dead. Someone killed him last night, maybe a few hours after you said you or one of your friends would get him. You told James Franzen and Eddie how to find Sokol."

Zembinsky's face was inches from Lieberman's now. Zembinsky smelled surprisingly clean, and his breath smelled like mint mouthwash.

"Cop or no cop," he whispered, "there's just you and me here, and I'm going through the door. You move over, or I put you down. Your word against mine. Maybe I'll just bite your fucking nose off."

They were too close together for the young man to see the punch coming. Lieberman's right hand shot out straight, short, and hard to Zembinsky's chest. Zembinsky staggered back, mouth open, gasping for breath, holding his chest. He was about to fall to the floor when he backed against the bed and sat.

"Will you guys shut up for God's sake," the man in bed

two called out. "Merv's giving money away."

"It's Bill Cullen," Lieberman called, still standing in the same spot in front of the door. "Not Merv Griffin."

"Who the hell cares?" called the curtained man.

Who the hell cares, Lieberman thought, waiting for Zembinsky to catch his breath. The young man was bruised, bandaged, and in pain from a new attack. There was no fight left in him. There might still be swagger. Zembinsky tried to talk. Nothing came out. He put his hands on the bed to steady himself, his eyes on the old cop who had done this to him.

Lieberman's hip flared up from the punch he had thrown. He was not in a good mood.

"What did you talk about?" Lieberman asked.

"You mean did I tell them to kill Sokol?" Zembinsky managed to get out.

"That's what I mean."

"And you expect me to just tell you if I did?"

"No, I expect you to lie. Tell me a lie. Then I go to Eddie and Franzen and ask them what they talked to you about and see if you were smart enough to set up a lie you all agree on. I get the phone cut off in this room and I put a cop on the door so you can't call them."

"Cops die, too," Zembinsky said, teeth gritted.

No longer Marlon Brando. Now he was Dan Duryea, straw and threat, no substance. A twig.

"Everybody dies, Z," said Lieberman. "Some people just do it later or better than others. So, you want to tell me a story?"

"No, I want a lawyer."

"I'm not arresting you. I'm just asking questions."

"I don't like the questions," said Zembinsky, breathing

a little better, no longer holding his hands to his chest. "I want to call my father. He's a lawyer."

"Suit yourself," said Lieberman. "Give me your father's number. I'll place the call. You talk, then the phone comes out."

"We didn't kill him," Zembinsky said, as Lieberman moved to the phone on the night table.

There was something in the way he said it that made Lieberman pause.

"We talked, me and Eddie, about how it had all turned to shit. We puffed. You know what I mean?"

"Bragged."

"Yeah, bragged, strutted, talked like assholes about how we were walking away from this one, what we'd do next, go to San Diego or something. We didn't talk about Sokol. That's the truth. Well, I did tell him Sokol and you and the other cop had come to see me. I didn't tell it the way it happened. We didn't talk about getting back at Sokol. That was just talk for you. I'm full of shit. Okay. You happy?"

"Eddie?" Lieberman asked.

Zembinsky was trying to find another actor to imitate, but he wasn't up to it. One punch and he had caved.

"I told him I was going to be okay and to keep his mouth shut if the cops came to see him. Nothing else. Dean's not a talker."

"He say anything?"

"He said he'd take care of things."

Zembinsky looked up at the television screen. A commercial for a Jean-Claude Van Damme movie was on. Lieberman waited for the young man to try to do a Belgian accent. Zembinsky didn't say anything.

People were laughing on the television set, laughing at a joke told twenty years ago by a dead man.

Lieberman picked up the phone.

"What's your father's number?"

The way to do it was to do it calmly, gently, quickly, and that is what Hanrahan did.

It was almost two in the morning when he rang the bell to the Sokol apartment. The building was in a ten-year-old fifteen-story high-rise on Sheridan Road across from the Loyola University campus. The number on the bell next to the name was 2C, probably not high enough to get a view of Lake Michigan over the university's trees and classroom buildings.

"Yes?" came a woman's voice on the intercom.

"Mrs. Sokol?"

"Yes?"

"Police. I'm Detective Hanrahan. Can I talk to you?"

"Arnold," she said flatly.

"Yes, it's about your husband."

"Is he with you?"

"No, Mrs. Sokol. Can I come up?"

"Is he in the hospital?"

"No, if I could . . ."

A buzzer rang, and Hanrahan moved to the door to open it. It was still buzzing as he stepped inside and found the elevator in front of him. It was only one flight up, but Hanrahan's knees were bone on bone and bore the scars of three operations to keep him functioning. Football had once been his life. It was long gone, but he didn't regret the loss, not anymore.

He stood in front of the door to 2C knowing the woman

was looking at him through the peephole. He stepped back, hands folded in front of him. He was wearing his sports jacket and a tie, which he had knotted on the elevator. He needed a shave, but not badly.

He was a formidable presence, broad-shouldered, holding his own in a battle of the bulge.

"Mrs. Sokol," he said softly, taking out his wallet and badge and holding it up where she might be able to see it.

Locks turned, and the door opened.

She stood there, plump, pale, maybe thirty-five, maybe older. She wore a green robe. Her hair was dark and short and as unkempt as it had been when he had seen her at the hospital when she had embraced her husband. Her eyes told Hanrahan that she knew.

He waited to be invited in but she simply stood in the doorway, one hand holding the top of her robe closed over her small breasts.

"Mrs. Sokol, I'm sorry to tell you this, but your husband is dead."

"Dead," she repeated.

"Yes, I'm sorry to tell you this. May I come in?"

"Dead," she repeated without moving.

Bill Hanrahan stepped forward, a single unthreatening step.

"May I come in?"

She looked down the carpeted hallway outside her apartment door to see if anyone else was there. Then she turned and walked back into the apartment, leaving the door open.

He followed her and found himself in a small, neat and comfortable, but not colorful, living room. There was a single light on, a table lamp next to a wooden entertain-

ment center with a television set and CD player against one
wall. In front of the windows sat a chair and desk with a
computer surrounded by neat file boxes. It was still dark.
He couldn't tell whether she could see the lake when dawn
came. He hoped she could.

Her back was to him, and he could see that she was
crossing herself. His hand started to come up, and he found
himself doing the same as she turned, revealing the cross
on the wall she had been facing.

"You're Catholic," she said.

"Yes."

"Was there a priest?"

Hanrahan hadn't thought about it. To him Sokol was a
confused Jew, but now he remembered that he had converted to please his wife.

"No," he said.

"We need a priest," she said. "Where is he? Where is
Arnold?"

"I . . . the morgue."

"Don't let them touch the body. Not till the priest gets
there."

She dashed barefoot to a white portable phone on a table
next to the pale blue sofa. She picked it up and handed it
to Hanrahan.

"Please," she said.

Hanrahan pulled out his wallet-sized address and phone
book, found the number, and called the morgue. He didn't
know the attendant who answered, but he identified himself and checked to be sure Sokol's body had arrived and
hadn't been touched.

"Won't get to him for hours, maybe not till tonight.
Backed up. Full moon. They say it's superstition, but I'm

here to tell you it's not. People go nuts with a full moon. People fall in love with their guns and knives and bottles they can break when the moon is round and white."

"I guess," said Hanrahan. "There's a priest on duty at Cook County Hospital."

"Always is," said the attendant.

"Victim named Sokol needs last rites," said Hanrahan. "Priest knows what to do."

"I'll page him," said the attendant.

"Thanks," said Hanrahan.

"Least I can do for the poor son of a bitch. Full moon. Believe in it."

"I do," said Hanrahan, and hung up. He turned to Mary Sokol, who was sitting in a blue armchair that matched the sofa. She was hugging herself, knees together.

"It's being done," he said.

"Oh my God," she said suddenly, jumping up, eyes wide. "He didn't commit suicide, did he?"

"No," said Hanrahan.

"What?" she asked, looking into his eyes for an answer.

"He was murdered, Mrs. Sokol."

"Arnold," she said. "Arnold."

She started to move back to the sofa, paused, and turned. "You want some coffee?"

He didn't, but he said that he did to keep her busy. She moved to the kitchen, and he followed her, waiting for the next question, the question that always came.

"I'll have to give you instant," she said, moving to a cupboard in the small kitchen. "Arnold grinds beans in the morning, makes it fresh. He's not really a coffee drinker. It's for me. We get it in the mail. Gevalia. You know them?"

"No, ma'am," he said.

"I can't grind. My children are sleeping. It might wake them, especially the baby, Luke. Matthew, he's six. He'd sleep through it, but . . ."

"I understand."

He sat at the round glass-topped table and waited while she microwaved water. There were file boxes on the table like the ones around the computer in the other room, but there was more than enough space to put down a few cups.

"I'm sorry about the mess," she said, looking at the file boxes. "I work at home. I do Internet research for authors, most professors at Loyola, a few at Northwestern, Roosevelt, even the University of Chicago."

She stood looking around the room as if she had never seen it before.

"You can find anything, almost anything on the Internet if you know how to . . . I'm sorry."

"No problem."

"Coffee? All I have is instant decaffeinated," she said.

"Decaffeinated is fine."

He waited. Sometimes they were numb. Sometimes they took a while, but it always came. It had to come. When she finally set the cup of coffee in front of him, she said, "He did it, didn't he?"

"He?" asked Hanrahan, putting the cup to his lips. It was bitter and not very hot.

"The man he owed the forty thousand dollars," she said.

"Forty thousand dollars?"

"Maybe more. I'm not sure. Business was bad. Arnold should have let it go, but it's been in the family for three generations. He . . . I'm sorry. I keep saying I'm sorry. I don't know what else to say."

"Who was this man your husband owed the money to?"

"He never told me. I don't know if . . . Wait."

She went through one of the doors, which led to the two bedrooms, and returned in a few seconds with a thin, black leather briefcase. She handed it to Hanrahan.

"I never opened Arnold's briefcase. He carried it with him everywhere. Maybe the man's name is in there, in his notebook or appointment book."

"May I take this?" asked Hanrahan.

She shook her head in what Hanrahan took for a "yes."

"It's my fault," she said. "I pushed him about so many things. I did . . ."

Hanrahan finished his coffee quickly.

"Could I have some more coffee, Mrs. Sokol."

"More . . . oh, coffee? Yes."

She took his empty cup and moved into the kitchen.

"Arnold is dead," she told the sink and herself. "Arnold is dead."

Wychovski had to squeeze past the huge man at the bottom of the stairwell. The man was big, black, and in a bad mood. His breath smelled of chicken and something sweet. It would have been easier if the big man had gone first, but that wasn't the way it was done, couldn't be, wouldn't make sense.

The black man wore black. Black cotton shirt with a button-down collar, black jeans, black shoes, black mood. He patted down Wychovski professionally, even went between his legs, stuffing a thick finger into his shoes. Finding the Glock in his sweatshirt was no problem. Wychovski had carefully pulled it out and handed it to him. The black man had pocketed it and gone on searching. He took out a handful of gold animals from Wychovski's pocket and dropped them back in. He nodded when he was satisfied, and they started up.

The stairs, wood, uncarpeted, creaked as Wychovski moved upward, feeling the weight of the big man behind him. At the top was a closed door. The stairway was dimly lit. The stairs were narrow. Two doors, narrow stairway. Even a fast raid would give Walter time to hide any immediate problems. Depending on his relationship to the man behind Wychovski, Walter could simply have the black man fill the doorway, calmly demanding to see a warrant, then slowly reading it. Fences, the smart ones, were prepared for such contingencies. Walter was a smart one. Maybe too damn smart for what Wychovski needed.

When he reached the top of the stairs the black man reached past him to open the door, and Wychovski stepped inside.

The room was huge. High ceilings. It looked like something out of one of the old *Architectural Digests* Wychovski had sometimes looked at in prison. Rooms with plush, tasteful furniture and views of forests in valleys below or the Golden Gate Bridge at night. This room had no view from the windows on either side. A brick wall left. A brick wall right. Dining room left, with a table big enough for a dozen people. Table looked like it had been built for King Arthur with high-backed dark hand-carved chairs with arms. The table was bare. Sideboards flanked it. A badly faded tapestry on one wall, a knight on a horse, sword pulled back, about to slash a two-headed dragon. The tapestry on the other wall was less faded and not violent, Madonna and child surrounded by women with smiles and men with beards.

The other half of the room was a square of not matched

but compatible antique furniture. Deep chairs with wooden arms. Two sofas. A big table in the middle with a bowl of flowers. The flowers were colorful, real. Against one wall was a gigantic television set in a massive carved cabinet whose doors were open but which could be closed to hide the screen that threw off the tone. This section of the room had paintings on the walls, four big ones, one of dogs on the hunt, one of a girl on a hill in a frilly dress with one hand on her hat to keep the wind from blowing it away, one of a forest with a river running through it, and one of a man with long hair and a knowing and evil smile.

"That's Count Ferdinand Devereaux," said Walter, who sat in a chair across from Wychovski, who was looking at the smiling man in the painting. Walter wore jeans that looked as if they had just come off the rack. They fit him perfectly. So did the pale blue T-shirt with the little pocket. "A real son of a bitch. A real Bugs Moran. Didn't like the way you looked at him, he ran you through or planned an elaborate torture and invited people to watch. Credited with doing in more than four hundred people, mostly in-nocent, but who knows. Violent man."

Walter was a lean man who kept himself in good con-dition. He must have been sixty, maybe more, but he didn't look it. Stuffed his face in ice water every morning. Worked out after a protein shake. Showered three times a day. He kept his head shaved and wore a full but not ex-cessive mustache. His hero was G. Gordon Liddy.

Everyone except street trash knew about Walter. Walter told them. Walter also told them straight out with no ne-gotiating what he would take and what he wouldn't and how much he would pay. Walter was an honest fence. Wal-ter was a tough fence.

"I plan to be in bed in ten minutes," Walter said, looking at his watch. "Ten, no more. And I'm not in a good mood. Today's not been one of my better days."

"Yesterday," said the black man standing behind Wychovski. "It's already tomorrow."

"Right," said Walter, nodding. "Technically, it's tomorrow. No, technically it's today. I was just talking about the period of time from the moment I got up in the morning with a stiff neck."

"I'm sorry to hear it," said Wychovski, thinking that no one could have had a worse day than he was having.

"Told you not to come here," Walter said calmly, reaching for a large mug of what was probably tea. It smelled strong, but not like coffee. Wychovski could suddenly smell everything in the big room, flowers, tea, the man behind him, the old wood, the cool air.

"What I've got you can melt down," Wychovski said. "I'm gone. I never heard of you. You know my word is good."

"I know your word is supposed to be good," said Walter. "But you've had a stupid busy day. Killed a cop. Killed a jeweler. Pryor's dead. No loss. You are not a good risk, and I don't need to take chances."

Wychovski plunged his hands into his pockets, pulling out little gold animals, a zoo full. He dropped them on the table in front of Walter and went back in for more. When he had fished the last scorpion from his pocket and wiped a speck of lint away, he stood back. It hadn't been much work, but he was having difficulty breathing.

Walter looked at the glittering pile, then past Wychovski to the black man. Wychovski didn't look back to see the man's reaction.

"The table you just dumped this menagerie on is fourteenth-century Dutch. If you've put one small scratch on it, you pay."

"I pay," Wychovski agreed. He would have agreed to anything. He wanted out. In the street, in the car he had felt desperate. He would do anything. He would walk out of here with cash no matter what he had to do. But right now he would settle for just walking out of here.

Walter reached over and picked up something that looked like an anteater. He fingered it, turned it over. Put it back. Picked up a lion, turned it over in his very clean hands and held it gently in his palm.

"They're good, very good," he said. "The man was an artist, George."

Wychovski wasn't happy about hearing his first name used by the fence. It implied something. He didn't know whether it was something good, bad, or indifferent.

"They're too good," Walter said. "Too good to melt down, but too good to sell anywhere but where they don't care and won't be spotted. You know where that is, George?"

George didn't know. George didn't care. George wanted out the door and down the stairs, walking, not being thrown. George Wychovski wanted money in his wallet, two or three cups of coffee, a different car, and the road to St. Louis.

"Singapore maybe," said Walter. "Hong Kong. Maybe some sheik in Saudi Arabia. The stuff is good, George. I'll not kid you on that. But the risk. The risk. Accessory to murder. A cop. I'll have to sit on this stuff for years. And the cops are going to come see me. Now, normally the cops, especially three friends in the district, are polite and willing to accept gifts, but a dead cop . . ."

He looked at Wychovski and drank some more tea, waiting for a response.

"You'll take them?"

Walter shrugged and put his hands behind his head, supposedly to show he was relaxed, actually to show his muscles. He looked at the rampage of tiny animals and said, "Three thousand."

Wychovski said nothing. If Walter was offering three thousand knowing how hot they were, knowing that a dead cop was involved, they were worth more, much more.

"They're worth a hundred thousand," Wychovski said, more than half expecting the big man to put an arm around his neck from behind and simply strangle him. Wychovski was in good shape, but he'd be no match for the black man.

"You're right," said Walter. "But I'm offering you three thousand. Listen, George. I could simply have Mr. Dickerson remove your head and dispose of your body and not give you a nickel. Then I wouldn't have to worry about what you might tell the police if they catch you, providing they let you live long enough to tell them anything. I'd just have to ask Mr. Dickerson to clean up the mess and dispose of the remains. You know what's keeping you alive?"

"Your generous heart," said Wychovski, trying to bluff it out, hoping he wasn't sweating, unable to check.

Walter shook his head no.

"My reputation is keeping you alive," he said. "You die, and somehow word gets out, who knows how, that I might

have been involved, I lose suppliers. Most suppliers, even
the ones with very, very bad habits, don't want to risk their
lives. So, three thousand, no, three thousand two hundred
dollars and you walk out of here and start running. I was
thinking of dropping the offer to two thousand and one,
make it a space odyssey for you, but I'll tell you the truth
George, this isn't a bad deal for me."

"I'll take it," Wychovski said.

Walter got up, went around the chair, and moved to a
door. He went through the door, closing it behind him.
Wychovski turned to look at the black man, Dickerson.
There was no expression on the man's face when his eyes
met Wychovski's.

Walter was back in a few seconds. He left the door open
behind him. The light was on in what looked like a bedroom. A safe was open. Walter wasn't worried. Walter was
carrying a tote bag, green with the word BELIZE in white
block letters.

"Fifties, twenties, a few hundreds," Walter said, handing
the bag to Wychovski. "Mr. Dickerson will show you out.
We'll remove the ammunition from your gun and he'll give
it back to you on the stairs. If this is the gun you used on
the cop . . ."

"It isn't," said Wychovski.

"Fine. Good-bye. We don't do business again. I don't
care if you walk in with the Crown Jewels, especially if you
walk in with the Crown Jewels. Anything else you can think
of?"

Wychovski said nothing.

"Anything you can think of, Mr. Dickerson?"

Mr. Dickerson responded by shooting Walter the fence
in the face and neck. Two shots, not much noise. Walter
fell face first in the mound of golden animals.

"I don't know. I'd say *shpilkes*," said Morris Hurvitz, holding his toasted everything bagel above his cup of coffee and trying to decide if dunking it was a good idea. Morris was short, bespectacled, and about to celebrate his eightieth birthday. He was also a psychologist with a loyal cadre of patients who would probably visit him in the cemetery and stand over his grave with a handful of flowers asking his advice.

Morris Hurvitz, Ph.D., was not the oldest, nor the most outspoken or even the unofficial leader of the group of old men who met daily at the T&L Deli on Devon Avenue. The Alter Cockers had their own table near the window and their morning numbers varied from three or four to as many as eight or even ten.

With the exception of Howie Chen, who had owned a Chinese restaurant a block away till he retired five years ago, the Alter Cockers were all Jewish. A few spoke Hebrew. A few others spoke anything from forty words to relatively fluent Yiddish. Howie's Yiddish, after half a century of dealing with Jewish customers in the obligatory

Chinese neighborhood restaurant, was more than forty words and far less than fluent but better than most at the table, including that of Morris Hurvitz. Howie had been shifting in his chair next to Morris Hurvitz, which had brought on the Hurvitz diagnosis of *shpilkes*, a less than clinical appraisal which meant that for unknown reasons the person with the affliction could not sit still.

"My grandson had a big day yesterday," explained Howie, whose fully round face showed concern.

"Congratulations," said Herschel Rosen, the table's acknowledged would-be comic, "he's finally moved his bowels. May we all join him."

"If I had my Mylanta, I'd toast to that," said Al Bloombach, who served as Herschel's second banana. Al was still called Red by his older friends though the hair that brought him the nickname was all but gone and certainly no longer red.

"Graduated, MIT," said Howie, watching Morris Hurvitz make the big decision and dunk his bagel in the cup of coffee.

"I couldn't be there," said Howie. "Doctor says I shouldn't miss a day of treatment."

Howie was being given radiation therapy for prostate cancer, a condition shared by approximately one-third of the Alter Cockers, all but one of whom admitted it. There was no question about Howie's recovery. That had been assured, but treatment had been an issue. Howie, at seventy-six, was a perfect candidate for surgery. He had opted instead for radiation after having been told privately by Lou Roth that the surgery had left him impotent. Now, having missed his grandson's graduation, he was having second thoughts.

Morris Hurvitz bit into his coffee-soaked bagel and made a face.

"Hurvitz," Herschel Rosen said, pointing a finger at him across the table, "how many times a week are you going to do that? How many years? You dunk your bagel, make a face. You know you're not going to like it."

"It always seems like a good idea and who knows, some day, my taste will change. You gotta take a chance sometimes."

"Why?" asked Herschel. "I took enough chances in my life. Now I order the same thing every day . . ."

"Lox omelette, toasted egg bagel with a shmeer of cream cheese and a cup of black," said Hurvitz. "Where's your sense of wonder?"

"I'm filled with wonder," said Herschel, a forkful of omelette in his hand. "I wonder about the *fercockta* Republicans, global freezing."

"Global warming," Roth corrected.

"You go away to Florida in the winter," said Hershel. "What the hell do you know?"

"You get to be our ages, and a sense of wonder comes from enjoying an omelette, not having a fight with your wife, and having a good bowel movement."

"Again with the bowel movements," said Hurvitz. "You need a few months of good analysis to deal with your infantile obsessions."

"Infantile?" asked Rosen. "*Moi.* My granddaughter says that. *Moi.* She thinks it's cute. I think she's cute, but she's spoiled rotten. Ah, here come Sergeants Friday and Gannon. They can solve the mystery."

Lieberman and Hanrahan stepped into the T&L together. It was a few minutes to ten. The morning breakfast crowd, which had dwindled since the neighborhood had become increasingly Indian, Korean, and Vietnamese was still sufficient to make the T&L profitable in the morning, but the conversation of the past had been sustained primarily by the Alter Cockers, who had chosen not to leave the neighborhood where they had grown old.

There were two people at the counter sitting on the red leatherette swivel stools. They were a couple, young, white. They were shabbily dressed and didn't look as if they were part of the neighborhood. Wanderers passing through, whispering.

"Lieberman," said Rosen. "Is it cute to say *moi*? I'm asking because you are our resident detective. You and County Cork."

Hanrahan was tired, in no mood for games, no mood to correct the prodding old man and engage him in his favorite activity, provocation and meaningless banter. He couldn't help himself. Rosen was old. Rosen thought he was funny. Rosen, in spite of the fact that he was an old Jew, reminded Bill Hanrahan of his own long-dead father who loved nothing more than a verbal joust.

"Kildare," said Hanrahan. "My people were from Kildare. Like the street."

"*Moi,*" Roth said.

The rear booth, which was Lieberman and Hanrahan's unofficial second office, was open. Maish, Abe's brother, who owned and ran the T&L, kept it open unless he had a full house. The detectives sat across from each other, Lieberman facing the window and the Alter Cockers, Hanrahan with his back to them.

"*Moi* is French," said Lieberman. "From a Frenchman in the proper context it is either a simple acceptance of responsibility or a small or large act of hubris. Coming from an American kid, it is a clichéd affectation picked up from television sitcoms reinforced by laugh tracks."

"A lecture," said Rosen, looking at the other Alter Cockers.

Maish, Nothing-Bothers-Maish, was behind the counter serving coffee to the young couple. Lieberman could see their faces now. They didn't seem to be having a good day. The young man appeared to be on the verge of tears. The woman, no, she was just a girl, with dark short hair that needed combing, was touching the back of his head, consoling him.

Their story was as clear to Lieberman as *moi*. The young man was strung out. If you had the cash, this wasn't a bad neighborhood to score drugs. There were better ones, but this one wasn't bad. You just had to have the cash, and the couple didn't look like they had it.

The girl's eyes suddenly met Lieberman's. She came up with an obviously false smile covering pain and desperation. Lieberman blinked his eyes and waited while Maish, who looked like an overweight bulldog, apron around his waist, looked their way.

"Bill?" he asked.

"Three scrambled with grilled onions and mushrooms, rye toast, coffee," Hanrahan answered.

Maish didn't bother to ask his brother what he wanted. Maish was under strict orders from Bess about what her husband could and could not eat. Maish, at five-foot eight weighed close to 255 pounds. Abe at five-seven hit 145 on a festive day. But it was the younger brother, Abe, who had the cholesterol problem.

Abe was drawn to the T&L. He was comfortable there.

He was a mile from the problems of home and almost two miles from the Clark Street Station, from which they had both just come after reporting to their boss, Lieutenant Alan Kearney. Neither Hanrahan, Lieberman, nor Kearney had slept much during the night. Hanrahan and Lieberman had been working. Each had managed a few hours' sleep. Kearney had slept fitfully in his office. He spent more and more time in his office, more and more nights. He looked haunted. He was still a handsome man at forty-three, but his face was not as healthy and his blue eyes seldom flashed. Kearney was a good cop, one who had been pegged to move up, quite possibly to the top, chief of police. He was being groomed when disaster struck. One night his former partner had murdered two people and barricaded himself on the roof, publicly blaming Kearney for seducing his wife. It wasn't true, but it made no difference. Other things went wrong that night. Kearney relived the possible options he hadn't chosen, reviewed and imagined and went on working.

"So," said Lieberman, pulling out his notebook. "Let's do it, Father Murph."

Doing it involved a simple process in which each man reviewed and assessed what the other man had done on whatever case he was working.

Behind Hanrahan, the Alter Cockers laughed, and Hurvitz said with some annoyance, "Enough already."

"Widow knows nothing about the three who roughed up her husband," said Lieberman, "but she immediately thought it might have something to do with some money he owed. Questions you've answered. Widow says Sokol was with her from the time she picked him up at the hospital till around eight, when he said he had to take care of something. He told her that he was going to see the people he owed money to and was going to cash in his insurance policy, or tell them that he was going to do it as soon as possible. She felt he was falling apart. She says she reassured him, told him it was alright, that she had learned from what had happened to him that it was more important to have him alive and well than to have his insurance money. She said she didn't know who he had borrowed the money from but that it was forty thousand. He had used it to pay overdue business debts."

"Or so he said," Hanrahan corrected.

"Or so he said, or so she says he said," Lieberman amended. "He did mention that he had to meet the man and wouldn't be back for a few hours. She thinks he said something like, 'He's a little loco, and he likes to talk, but I'm sure he'll be reasonable. Don't worry I'm going to give the dog his money.' And . . . 'loco,' 'likes to talk,' 'lends money.' "

"Could be plenty of people," said Hanrahan, "except here's his appointment book. His wife gave me his brief-case. I found it inside."

He handed the small black book to Lieberman, who opened it.

"There's an entry for two weeks ago at six on a Tuesday, last week on Monday, and yesterday for nine. Doesn't say A.M. or P.M."

Lieberman put on his glasses and flipped to the most recent entry.

"El Perro," said Hanrahan.

Lieberman flipped through the book, checking the other dates. Neatly inked in little block letters the words "El Perro" appeared where Hanrahan had told him to look.

Abe glanced at a few other entries, all kinds of names and notations. All in the same neat block letters.

"I wouldn't want to owe your amigo money, Rabbi."

Lieberman's "amigo," Emiliano "El Perro" Del Sol, was known to have beaten Syvie Estaban nearly to death with a telephone for talking while Julio Iglesias was singing on the radio. El Perro was reported to have cut the throat of one of the Vargo brothers for accidentally stepping on his shoes. More than one person Lieberman knew had been in the Dos Hermanos bar the night El Perro beat into pleading senselessness two construction workers who dared look at him while he was painfully and slowly composing a letter to his mother. El Perro was the leader of the Tentaculos, the gang that believed it owned North Avenue and probably did.

El Perro was average only in height. He was lean, kept his hair cut short, and bore a white scar on his face from an incident Lieberman knew nothing about and did not want to know. El Perro was also clearly psychotic. He leapt from obsession to obsession and criminal enterprise to criminal enterprise. He was into selling protection, drugs, stolen goods, extortion, and occasional loan sharking. Few of those who borrowed from El Perro were the Mexicans, Central Americans, and Puerto Ricans who lived in his territory. The consequences of missing a payment were far worse than facing any creditor.

Lieberman and the Tentaculos' leader were not exactly friends though the line was thin. Lieberman had done favors for the gang leader in exchange for information and occasional assistance when Abe felt the law did not equal justice. The two men also shared a passion for the Chicago

Cubs. El Perro was especially passionate about Hispanic players, and once seriously considered issuing a threat to the ball club's owners not to trade any more Hispanic players unless it was for other Hispanics. Sammy Sosa was a God. Lieberman was a tough old Jew cop who spoke pretty good Spanish and couldn't be intimidated. Most recently El Perro had taken over a bingo parlor on North Avenue, where he set up his desk on the platform and did business. On Tuesday, Thursday, and Saturday nights he usually called the numbers himself.

The relationship between the cop and the gang leader had made the news twice, once in a *Chicago Tribune* story about Chicago cops and their criminal contacts, and once in the *Tribune* and *Sun-Times* and on the six o'clock news when Lieberman testified in court giving one of the Tentaculos named Machito a solid alibi for the murder of a rival gang member. Lieberman had told the truth. He had been with El Perro getting information on another homicide when the gang member had been murdered, and Machito had been present at the meeting.

Lieberman knew Internal Affairs had a file on him with a list of questionable shootings and associations with known criminals. It was part of the reason Abe had never been promoted, but just part of the reason.

"Maybe it's something else."

"Maybe."

"But we're going to find out."

"That we are," said Hanrahan, as Maish placed a large plater with a still-simmering omelette in front of him along with toast and coffee.

In front of Lieberman he placed a coffee and a large

bowl of oatmeal. Lieberman put his glasses back in his pocket and handed the appointment book back to his partner.

"One bagel, plain, toasted," said Lieberman.

"No. Take your business to Walgreen's."

"Walgreen's doesn't have bagels," said Lieberman, looking at the steaming bowl of gray cereal.

Maish shrugged, and Lieberman looked at his partner's omelette with his starving beagle eyes.

No one made a better omelette than Terrell, the short-order cook at the T&L. But it wasn't just omelettes. Terrell, whom Abe had convinced his brother to hire a dozen years earlier, had learned his skills in prison, where Abe had been largely responsible for his five-year stay. Terrell had found his true calling behind the walls. He was a cook. Jewish cooking had become his specialty, and he was brilliant at it, too brilliant at the moment for Abe, who longed for a slice of brisket or just one stuffed cabbage. There was a small blackboard on the wall near the passway to the kitchen. On the board were listed the daily specials. Lieberman tried not to look, but he didn't have the willpower. Cherry blintzes. It was more than a human being should be expected to endure.

Maish hovered. Abe sighed and reached for the sugar.

"I put sweetener in it already," Maish said. "Stevia."

"I appreciate your concern," said Abe, picking up his spoon. "Now if you'll let me down my medicine in peace."

"The temple caterers are going to handle the bar mitzvah dinner," said Maish.

"They're kosher," said Abe.

They had been over this a dozen times. Abe took a

spoonful. It wasn't bad. It wasn't a cherry blintz, but it wasn't bad.

"Who cares?" asked Maish. "Terrell can outcook all the kosher kitchens."

Abe and Bill ate silently. Maish went on.

"You're worried about Labal and Aviva?" Maish asked.

Labal and Aviva were the Lieberman brothers' ultra-Orthodox cousins from Brooklyn. There wasn't even a certainty that they would make it, let alone their combined total of sixteen children.

"God's gonna have a conniption fit because they don't eat kosher?" Maish went on. "We tell them it's kosher. I'll tell them. They'll have committed no sin. The dinner will cost you nothing instead of two thousand dollars."

"Three thousand," Abe amended. "I'd know it wasn't kosher. Bess would know. Yetta would know. They"—he nodded at the Alter Cockers—"would know."

"They'll all shut up," said Maish.

Maish was itching for a battle with God. Ever since his son David had been murdered by robbers and his pregnant daughter-in-law shot in the robbery, Maish had entered into battle with God. It wasn't that he didn't believe. He just didn't like God and was more than willing to take him on and accept the consequences.

Maish didn't know the full truth of his son's death. Abe did. So did Bill. There was no chance either one of them would ever tell, so they ate and listened just as the congregation of Mir Shavot had to listen to Maish, who doggedly attended services and forced the patient but besieged Rabbi Wass to deal with the bulldog of a man and his challenges.

"Maish, you want to do a dinner, wonderful. Do it on

the Sunday," said Abe. "I'd like that. I'd love it. I'd celebrate by eating piles of chopped liver and a half ton of
brisket, but Friday and Saturday we go kosher."

"God is a pain in the ass," said Maish, turning away from
the table. "And you can tell him I said so."

"You just told him," Abe said.

Maish disappeared into the kitchen.

"He's getting better," said Hanrahan.

"Yeah."

Suddenly Maish was at the table again looking not at his
brother but at Bill Hanrahan.

"You going to marry Iris or you're not?" asked Maish.

"I am."

"When?"

"Thursday," said Bill.

"Good, I'll cater a dinner. Abe and Bess's house. Unless
you're going to have Chinese."

"Catered Jewish will be fine with Iris," said Bill.
"Thanks."

"Someone appreciates reality at this table," Maish said,
heading back for the kitchen without looking at his
brother.

"Iris's father's giving us a party at the Black Moon the
night before," Hanrahan said softly. "Invitations will be in
the mail in a few days. What about James Franzen and
Edward Denenberg and our battered Melvin Zembinsky?"

"What about indeed."

"They sound as good as whoever Sokol went to see last
night," said Hanrahan, continuing to eat. "Well, almost as
good."

"We'll pay them each a visit. We've got a busy day."

Lieberman finished his oatmeal. Hanrahan was still eating. Maish was giving the young couple their third or fourth cup of coffee, and the Alter Cockers were debating the current state of the Israeli/Palestinian conflict.

"Be right back," said Hanrahan, rising and wiping his mouth with a napkin.

"You just inhaled a four-egg omelette," said Lieberman.

Hanrahan ignored him and headed for the men's room. There was half a bagel with cream cheese left on the side dish across the table. Lieberman was sure he could down it in no more than forty-five seconds.

"Please, sir," he said, looking toward his brother and holding up his bowl, "can I have some more?"

Maish nodded and turned to Terrell. The young girl was off the stool and moving toward Abe quickly.

"Hi," she said, standing over him and smiling.

There was a slight yellow to her teeth, but her skin was good, primarily because she was young, very young.

"Hi," he said.

"I waited till your friend was gone," she said.

Lieberman looked at the young man she had left at the counter. He was busy paying no attention. Lieberman was afraid he knew what was coming in addition to oatmeal.

"Wait," said Lieberman, reaching for his wallet.

She stood waiting and glanced back at the young man, who continued to act as if all this had nothing to do with him.

"I can do lots of things," she said softly. "You have a car?"

"Here," Lieberman said, handing her the card he had managed to pull from a small stack he kept near his cash.

She took the card and looked at it.

"I'm a cop. If a young lady were to solicit for prostitution, I'd be obligated to arrest her. I don't always meet my obligations, and I've got a busy day, so let's say you've hit a small piece of good luck. You from out of town?"

"Yeah," she said, clearly confused. "You're really a cop."

"It's my winning nature," said Lieberman. "That card is for a drug rehab center four blocks from here. Methodists run it. It's a good place. My name's on the back. Use it. They'll give you a place to spend a few days and some food and start you on a program. What've you got to lose?"

She looked at the card, reading it slowly. She'd probably give it to her boyfriend, and there was a chance they would stop in at the New Christian Center to at least pick up a meal and spend the night. It would give Dave Mahan, the minister, a shot at them. Dave was damn good. It was a shot.

"We're from New Orleans," she said. "New Orleans, Louisiana."

Lieberman nodded. Maish came over with a fresh bowl of hot oatmeal. Hanrahan returned from the men's room, and the girl went back to her boyfriend at the counter.

"That what it looked like?" asked Hanrahan.

"It was."

"She wouldn't have tried it on me."

"You look like you might be a cop. I look like a guy who might own a pawnshop or a dry-cleaning store."

"I left temptation in your path, Rabbi," Hanrahan said, nodding at the slice of bagel.

"And I resisted," said Lieberman, looking at the young man and woman, who were discussing the card she had handed to him. They looked over at the two policemen and hurried out of the T&L.

"Like a good recovering addict," said Hanrahan, picking up the slice of bagel.

Hanrahan was a recovering alcoholic. He knew what he was talking about, and Lieberman understood.

"I've joined cholesterol anonymous," said Lieberman, spooning up oatmeal. "We start each session standing up and reciting our pledge: I eat all the wrong food. I'm blocking my arteries. I'm letting my craving get in the way of my staying alive and taking care of myself and my loved ones. With your help and the help of Jesus, I will resist."

"Doesn't sound like a bad idea to me. Maybe you should start a group. You can substitute 'God' for 'Jesus' and you . . ."

The cell phone in Lieberman's pocket began to vibrate. He took it out and said: "Lieberman."

Then he listened, his eyes on his waiting partner. He took out his pen and began making notes on his pad, then he listened some more before saying, "We'll head right over."

He pressed a button, and the call ended.

"Gonna be a very long day, Father Murph," he said. "The other dead guy in the lake, Pryor. Did time in Federal and State. Strong arm. Not smart. Place he hit in Northbrook. Stole a bunch of gold animals like the one we found in his pocket. Three more were found about an hour ago in the apartment of Walter Crest."

"The fence."

"The fence," Lieberman agreed. "Walter is dead. Walter is very messy dead. Now we have a dead policeman and a dead fence and a dead ex-con tied together with a charm bracelet."

They both got up. They didn't try to pay Maish. Maish had made it clear long ago that any offer of payment from either his brother or Hanrahan would offend him.

They both waved at Terrell, who leaned out of the pass-way from the kitchen and whispered, "Maish is in the back taking in a load of smoked fish and lox."

He held out a paper bag. Lieberman hurried behind the counter to take it from him and quickly returned to his partner's side.

"You drive," Lieberman said.

They had come in an unmarked 1998 police vehicle, a tan Mustang.

Hanrahan shook his head and opened the door.

"So you're having a bar mitzvah?" Herschel Rosen called out.

"Had one about forty-seven years ago," said Lieberman. "Thought I'd try another."

"Who's catering?" asked Roth, winking at all the Alter Cockers.

"Mama Lina," said Lieberman. "Kosher pizza and cal-zone. You'll get your invitations."

"Tell her to make one with lox," shouted Howie Chen.

"Kosher lox pizza," said Rosen. "A new delicacy, could become a new bar mitzvah tradition. We should pass it on to the caterer."

In the car, driving toward toward Western Avenue, Abe opened the paper bag. No doubt. A cherry blintz. Two of them.

"You want one, Murph?"

"To keep you from eating it," Hanrahan said, reaching out his hand.

"You're a generous and good-hearted man," said Lieberman, wrapping a large warm blintz in one of the napkins and handing it to his partner.

"I'm up for beatification next year," said Hanrahan. "Since Mother Teresa died they've been looking for some-one like me."

"You've got my vote," said Lieberman, taking his first bite from the delicacy in his hand.

"And we've got a tail," said Hanrahan. "Four cars back. Dark blue Buick with tinted windows."

"See him," said Lieberman, looking in the side view win-dow and chewing. "Life is interesting, Father Murphy."

"Indeed it is, Rabbi. Indeed it is."

Melvin Zembinsky had dressed and made it to the door of the hospital room without falling on his face. It hadn't been easy. The room and the floor did not cooperate. They fun-house wavered and wobbled. His mother and father had called. They had met the night before with the doctor, a Pakistani named Bandhari, who advised that their son remain in the hospital for another day or two of testing. They had agreed. Z had not, but he had said nothing.

He had called Eddie and asked him to come to the hospital to get him. Eddie had a part-time job as a telecom salesman. Eddie had a '93 Toyota. He agreed to be there at ten, in front of the hospital entrance.

Z checked his wristwatch. He had about eleven minutes to make it. He strongly considered going past his bed, pushing back the curtain, taking the remote away from the old fart in the next bed, and turning off the goddamn game-show channel forever. But it was easier just to get the hell out.

He moved slowly, went through the door, tried to stand up straight and look normal, which was difficult with a bandaged head, a sore back that bent him over, and a bloodshot left eye. But hell, this was a hospital. What did you expect to see in a hospital?

I expect maybe to see a cop is what I maybe expect, thought Z, keeping his eyes down as he moved past the nursing station and headed for the elevators. No one stopped him. No cop appeared.

Z was sure of lots of things. Life sucked. There was no God. His parents saw him as a disappointment and a burden, and he did not kill the guy who had put him in the hospital. Sokol, Arnold Sokol.

He pressed the button for the elevator. A woman, who looked a little like his mother only not as well dressed, joined him and waited. He watched the white lights. The elevators were on the first and fifth floors.

If he didn't kill Sokol, that made the odds pretty good that it had either been Jamie or Eddie. He had talked to both of them, told them of Sokol's attempt to kill him, told him about the two cops and the crazy rabbi. He hadn't called Jamie this morning, and when he called Eddie he did not tell him what that little Jew cop with the creepy eyes had said about Sokol being murdered. Z wanted whichever one of them who did it to tell him. He was sure they would. Maybe not directly. They were both too smart for that, but they would let something drop, strut, brag, smirk. Eddie was the most likely, the most violent. Eddie didn't think about tomorrow. Shit, he didn't even think about later today.

Z made it to the lobby and the front of the hospital with three minutes to spare. He felt as if he were going to throw up and wondered if he should do it in the flower bed a few feet away or get into Eddie's car and tell him to stop when they cleared the hospital. If he threw up here, they might drag him back in.

His goddamn head hurt. Sokol was the asshole who had done this to him and in front of Jamie and Eddie. Sokol deserved a hard one in the head from behind with a Coke bottle. Not enough to kill him but enough to make him spend the rest of his life worrying about Coke bottles from behind.

Eddie pulled up. Z managed to move forward, open the car door, and slide in. Eddie's car smelled like stale pizza.

"Get away from here and stop somewhere," said Z.

"Where?" asked Eddie.

"Just drive before I puke all over your fucking car," said Z.

Eddie stepped on the gas. He was the biggest of the three friends and, at twenty, the oldest. He lived alone in a rusting trailer behind a house in Chicago on North Rockwell. The trailer was small, but cheap. It was their unofficial party and planning space. There wasn't much to it, and it was usually filthy, but no one bothered them. They certainly bothered others, but neighbors were not inclined to complain, though once while they were drunk and blasting heavy metal at about two in the morning, two BB holes went through one of the trailer's windows. They had tried to go out in search of the shooter, but knew they were in no shape for a chase.

Eddie's phone had rung about ten minutes later. Eddie had passed out. Jamie was shaking his head to the beat. Jamie didn't like Eddie's trailer. He hated the filth and the bugs he sometimes saw, but he could get over it by downing three or four beers. When the phone had rung that night, Z answered. A frightened, angry man's voice said,

"That was just the first shots in this war. I'm going to shoot your damn trailer to pieces unless you stop the noise."

"And," Z had answered, "you stupid fuck, I've got caller ID, and I know your goddamn phone number."

It was a lie, but Z could tell from the man's voice that it would make him squirm. The BB sniper had hung up. He was probably still sitting there, weeks later, waiting for a call in the middle of the night or the three friends to come out of an alley when he came home some night and beat the shit out of him. Yes, there had been good times. But this was not one of them.

"You sick?" asked Eddie, driving.

Z looked at him. Eddie was bald, skinhead shaved with a small blue tattoo of a throwing knife in the center of his head. He figured if he ever wanted to look straight, all he would have to do was let his hair grow in. He had a baby face and a decent body, and he worked out when he wasn't drunk or trying to sell people things on the phone that they didn't want or need.

Eddie wore tight T-shirts to show off his muscles, which weren't exceptional, nowhere near as impressive as Jamie's. Eddie had capped teeth and a good smile, but he smelled, and had no line to pick up or deal with women. So, except for Skank Lilly at the Woodburn Bar on Ashland, he got no sex except what he paid for.

Eddie's passion was exotic weapons. He was a survivalist. There were times when Z had to tell him to shut up about blowguns, knife fighting, and killer martial arts.

Eddie's trailer was filled with books and magazines. They piled up in and around his bed. *Zips, Pipes and Pens, Deadly Blowguns: How to Make and Use Them, The Art of Throwing Weapons, How to Make a Silencer for a .22, Thai Boxing*

Dynamite. Paladin Press catalogs were piled high next to the toilet. Eddie read them all. He never used anything he read in his ragged library. Jamie, big and dumb, who read nothing but worked out constantly, could break Eddie with one hand. Even Z could take Eddie out without any sweat, but Eddie was always willing to go along with whatever Z wanted to do, and he wasn't worried about hurting people when it seemed like fun.

"Just fucking pull over," Z said.

Eddie pulled over in front of a house with a driveway. There were no cars in the driveway. Z grabbed some Wendy's yellow napkins from the dashboard and stepped out of the car on weak legs. He leaned over to vomit on the grass. No one was out on the street. Z wiped his mouth with the Wendy's napkins and threw them on the lawn. Then he got back in the car and Eddie took off.

"The Colonel can clean it up," said Eddie.

"Wendy's is Dave. The Colonel is Kentucky Fried. The Colonel is dead. Dave is dead. Know anyone else dead?"

Eddie looked puzzled and said, "No. I mean lots of people. My mother. My Aunt Joannie."

"More recent," said Z, feeling better but tasting bitter acid. "I need a drink, a Coke."

"Okay."

Z looked at Eddie, who looked back at him.

"Sure you're okay?"

"Perfect. Sokol."

"Who?"

"The guy on the rocks. The guy who put me in the hospital. The guy I talked to you about last night."

They drove south heading toward Chicago.

"Bastard," Eddie said. "We gotta find him."

Z looked at Eddie, looked hard.

"What?" asked Eddie. "What are you looking at?"

No, not Eddie. Eddie was not a total idiot, but he wasn't good enough to be pulling off this act. That left Jamie.

Z made a decision. The hell with Jamie. What the hell was Jamie to him? He would throw Jamie to the cops. He and Eddie together. Jamie was big, blond, drew the girls, but he was stupid, stupid and strong. Until a few minutes ago, Z didn't think Jamie Franzen had it in him to kill. If Jamie did it, Z was going to turn him in and save his own ass. Z had an alibi. He was in the hospital. He knew nothing about it. He could even say he called Jamie and told him to leave Sokol alone but Jamie said he wouldn't. The world was full of Jamies and Eddies and, yes, Z's, too, but *this* Z wasn't going to go down for a murder. They could have Jamie's ass and all his holes in prison in Marion.

"I'll stop at Wendy's on Western," said Eddie.

"Where's Jamie?"

"Jamie? I don't know. Maybe sleeping."

"Let's go wake him up."

Wychovski wondered why he was still alive.

"Here," said Dickerson, handing him a Big Mac from the bag in the black man's lap.

Wychovski took it. The car smelled like french fries and fat. Wychovski looked at the suitcase Dickerson's feet were resting on. It was filled with cash from Walter's safe. Who knew how many thousand. Maybe a million. All unmarked.

Staying alive was number one on Wychovski's agenda. Number two, if he made it that far, was getting that case away from the man who munched a quarter pounder with cheese next to him.

Wychovski was driving a Lexus, a black almost new
Lexus. He had never driven anything this smooth before.
If he ever got that cash, he could buy himself one. He
wouldn't keep this one. This one, Dickerson had said, belonged to Walter. He had told Wychovski not to worry,
that the car wasn't in Walter's name, but one of his nieces.
Still, step by step by step.

Stay alive. Get the money. Get the hell out of town.
Drive southwest or southeast. Rent a furnished room. Sit
tight for four or five months. Get new ID. That was far
enough ahead to think.

But to accomplish this it was pretty clear he would have
to kill Dickerson, who sat within easy reach of the same
shotgun, now reloaded, that he had used to tear Walter
into red meat.

"I've been waiting for someone like you for almost a
year," Dickerson said.

Wychovski said nothing. He followed directions. Dickerson told him where to go. He went. South and west.
Past the old United Center where Michael Jordan had
played, deep into a run-down black West Side.

"Racist bastard always kept the door closed when he
opened the safe, always reset the alarm," Dickerson went
on. "I played good nigger, tough nigger, loyal nigger. He
paid well, but I wanted more. Know what I mean?"

"I know," said Wychovski.

A Lexus in Lawndale with a white guy driving. But he
had Dickerson riding shotgun, and he knew Dickerson was
not afraid to shoot.

"I waited. You came. Old Walter made a mistake. Last
mistake. Maybe his only mistake besides his wardrobe.
You've got a question."

"No," said Wychovski.

"Another burger?"

"No, thanks," said Wychovski.

"Coke?"

"Sure."

Dickerson handed him a container of Coke with a straw.

"You're thinking, 'Why didn't he kill me, too?' Right?"

"No," said Wychovski. "I was thinking why don't me and Dickerson team up. We'd make a good team."

Dickerson ate a pair of fries and shook his head.

"I don't need a partner, and with this," he said, patting the suitcase, "I won't need one for a long time. They're going to start looking for me. May take them a while, but they can probably do it, or maybe do it. No, I gotta show up and tell them what happened."

"What happened?" asked Wychovski.

"You came in, killed Walter," said Dickerson. "Sure you don't want another burger? Got a double cheese left."

"No, thanks. I killed Walter, took his money, and ran?"

"Back a step," said Dickerson. "Mind if I listen to the radio?"

"No," said Wychovski.

Dickerson reached over and pushed some buttons. Sixties rock came on. Dickerson turned down the volume, and said, "You killed a cop last night, killed a jewelry store guy, came with your pockets full of little gold wolves and such, and tried to make a deal. You had the shotgun. I was surprised. You blasted poor old Walter, took the money in his pocket, and took me hostage."

Wychovski had watched Dickerson fill the suitcase with cash and lock the safe. The money was free and clear.

"So," Dickerson went on, "if I blasted you back in Walter's now redecorated apartment, I'd have to hide all this money."

"Why am I taking you hostage?" Wychovski asked. "Why didn't I just kill you, too?"

"I'm working that out," said Dickerson with a smile. "I'll tell you when I do. I'm not sure whether you're gonna kill yourself or get jacked on the street. But you'll have the shotgun."

"And you?"

"I escaped. Jumped out of the car when you came to a stop. Ran to the phone and hit nine-one-one. Good citizen. Mayor'll give me an award maybe. Nah, but I've got my reward. Any more questions?"

"No," said Wychovski.

He was wearing a seat belt. His door was locked. He was sweating. Smell of fried meat and fat stronger. Smell of himself in fear. Shotgun out of reach. Dickerson's hands full. Fries in one. Burger in the other.

Woman walking a buggy with two little ones on one side of the street, Roosevelt Road. A cluster of winos outside a storefront bar named Willie's. The "W" in Willie was faint against the dark glass. The "illie" still stark and white.

Wychovski went through it in his mind. It was just past dawn. It was just about too late. He went over it in his mind like a bowler imagining his moves, a great free throw shooter seeing what he was going to do. There was a light. He stopped. Now. Who knew where Dickerson was taking him, how soon he would die if he just kept driving. Now.

He took his left hand off the wheel, and said, "Supposing we . . ."

He pushed the button on the door with his left hand, hit the seat-belt buckle button with his right, pushed the door open, and took his foot off the brake as he rolled into the street.

Dickerson and the Lexus shot forward. Bruises, not bad, knee was going to hurt, but Wychovski rolled and got to his knees as the Lexus sailed into the front of a condemned building with a closed store on the corner. The Lexus, driver's side door open, hit at about twenty miles an hour.

Nothing exploded. Nothing burned. Nothing but the car was damaged. If you don't count Dickerson, who came out of the car limping, shotgun in one hand, suitcase in the other, tan slacks stained with spilled Coke.

Wychovski stood up and ran. He didn't know where he was running. He ran down the street. It looked as if it should be a busy street, but it was still early.

Dickerson fired. A storefront window, hardware store, shattered, spraying glass. Wychovski ran, covered his head to ward off the sharp rain that cut into the backs of his hands and his scalp.

He hadn't been hit. He was still running, not fast, but running. He was in reasonably good shape. He had the feeling from Dickerson's body that the man behind him was in even better shape even though he might be limping. Better shape, determined, and closing in on him.

A pair of well-dressed black children, a boy and a girl no more than six, holding hands watched the bleeding white man run by. Wychovski saw no fear in their faces. Maybe cars crashed here every day. Maybe people were gunned down on the street here every morning. Maybe they talked about it in school. The little boy would raise his hand, and say, "Ms. Holmes, we seen a white man get blown up on the way to school this morning." And Ms. Holmes would answer, "That's interesting, Ronnie. Why don't you draw us a picture for the bulletin board."

A space between two buildings on his right. Another shotgun blast. Had the kids stepped back into a doorway? Were they cut into pieces? Would Ms. Holmes not get her report?

Wychovski was safe for the second inside the passageway. He ran. It was narrow. He had to run sideways over broken bottles, garbage, more smells, shit smells. Dying in this alley, having to fall into this. No. He moved as fast as he could. All Dickerson would have to do was turn the corner and fire. Couldn't miss. A door on the left. Wychovski put his back against the right wall and kicked at the door, kicked hard, kicked for his life. The door creaked. The hinges gave way. He jumped into darkness hearing Dickerson's footsteps hurrying down the narrow passageway.

Wychovski groped, saw light under a door, tripped over a box, got up fast, kicked the box back toward the door he had come through. He was in a storefront room. Counters, shelves with nothing much on them. Cots. People in them. All black faces looking at him in fear. A family? Mother, father, three kids in cots lined up next to each other.

Wychovski ran to the front door, threw the bolts, and opened it, jumping into the street. The same street where the Lexus sat snub-nosed. People were opening its doors and taking whatever they could carry. Radio, seats.

He turned right and ran. Getting tired now. Followed by the Terminator. The Black Terminator. He ran. Came to a corner. Turned right, glancing over his shoulder. No sign of Dickerson.

———

Side street. A few people passing him going to work or to nowhere. A running white man. White man with bloody scratches on his hands. The play of the day. Eighty yards to the next corner.

He made it. Touchdown. Six points and still alive. What was that football movie with Al Pacino where the guy's eye popped out during the game and they put it in a plastic bag? *Any Given Sunday.* But was this Sunday? No. Maybe. It was Wednesday. Maybe Tuesday. He wasn't sure.

This street was even smaller. A few people were coming and looked at him. Would they give him away? He ran up a concrete stairway, holding the rusting iron railing of a three-story brick house. An old woman with a big white purse in her hand looked at him. She wore thick glasses and a white dress with big blue flowers on it.

"Hide me," he panted.

"Police after you?"

"Crazy man with a shotgun," he managed to get out.

The woman stepped back to let him enter and closed the door after him. He put his back to the hallway wall and pushed closed the curtains on the window next to the door. Then he pushed them back just a bit. Pushed them back far enough to see Dickerson turn the corner and look both ways, shotgun in his right hand.

The old woman's face was next to his, peering through enormous lenses.

"That's him," Wychovski said. "He stole my money and my car and he wants to kill me. I ran away."

He looked out the window again. Dickerson couldn't decide which way to go. He looked right and then left. As his eyes turned toward the house where Wychovski was,

Wychovski pulled the woman away from the curtain. He stood breathing hard for five or six seconds, then looked again. Dickerson was gone.

"We'd best call the police," said the old woman. "Come with me."

Wychovski followed her, amazed to be alive, wondering how he would keep her from calling 911.

The universe is very large, he said to himself. And life is very hard.

The two detectives who caught the case were happy to cooperate with Lieberman and Hanrahan. Hell, they were happy to turn the whole damn thing over to them.

On the green board in their captain's office was a list of open homicide cases. It was a long list. The only things that made it shorter from time to time was the apprehension and arrest of a suspect or the fact that more space was needed on the board so that the oldest cases went from the board but stayed on the computer.

Williams and Bustero had their names next to the most open cases on the board. Had they any hope of catching the killer that day, they would have entered into some kind of give-and-take, but they weren't working with much confidence lately. Williams was young, lean, black, and good-looking enough to be a news anchor. He was even dressed like one, in a well-pressed navy blue suit and a red tie. Bustero was short, homely, and a few years older than Bill Hanrahan. Bustero had no place up the ladder to go, and his rumpled jacket and slacks, cop belly, and open collar made it clear he had no illusions.

Chicago was averaging about two murders a day this year. The number had been going down slowly but steadily for years if the police department wasn't playing too loose with the figures.

That was the good news. The bad news was that over the past decade, the police were able to solve just over 40 percent of those murders. When the number of murders was high back in the eighties, the clearance rate had hit 76 percent. If you added in the old murder cases, some dating back a dozen years, that were cleared, you started approaching a 50 percent clearance rate.

Which meant, simply, that half the murderers in Chicago got away with it. Detroit and Los Angeles were just as bad.

The department said the problem lay with overworked detectives, undertrained detectives, too many new detectives coming in to replace veterans who walked out the door the minute they hit pension age. More and more were taking early retirement.

And so, Bustero and Williams knew their captain would be only too happy to turn the case over to someone else.

Only one thing stopped them from just walking away.

They stood in the big room where Walter the Fence lay dead. Actually, he was reclining on a bloodstained sofa. The wall and the paintings behind him were Jackson Pollack sprayed with the blood and brain matter from the dead fence.

Williams held the palm of his right hand up and open in front of Lieberman and Hanrahan. Resting in it were two small gold figures, one a snake, the other a possum.

"Hansel," said Hanrahan. "Leaves a trail for us. Think he wants to be caught?"

"I think he killed a cop," said Bustero. "I think the case

is yours, but unofficially we stay on it and it stays off our
board. Suit you?"

"Suits us," said Lieberman. Someday he and Hanrahan
might need a similar favor.

"Tell us what you need," said Bustero.

Lieberman watched as the crime scene people puttered,
printed, sampled, and scraped with gloved hands and plastic zipper bags.

Lieberman told them about Pryor.

"He did time in Stateville. Armed robbery. We'd like
names and photographs of people he knew there who are
on the street, people he knew well. Might be something.
Might not. Then you take a trip out to Northbrook with
whatever you get and show the pictures to the widow. See
if she can identify any of them. The widow's description
and the one from the dead cop's partner say Hansel is
white, maybe mid- to late forties, a little chunky, graying
hair."

Williams and Bustero nodded.

"We'll dig," said Bustero. "Give me your number."

Hanrahan gave him a number. Bustero wrote it in pencil
on a napkin he pulled from his pocket.

"One thing is screwy here," Bustero said as Abe and Bill
started to leave. "Walter had a wallet full of cash, more
than two thousand dollars. Our guy comes here to sell his
animals, blows Walter away, doesn't take his ready cash,
leaves a trail."

"Who's Walter's hooligan?" asked Lieberman.

"Black guy named Dickerson," said Williams before his
partner could be politically correct and label Dickerson
"African-American." Williams didn't see himself as African-
American. He was American. He was black. Well, actually

he was a light chocolate brown, but he was more black than his partner was white. Bustero was a pale pink. No one identified perps as Italian-Americans, Jewish-Americans, Russian-Americans, Venezuelan-Americans.

"Dickerson have a record?" asked Lieberman.

"Odds are good," said Bustero. "We'll find him."

"Well, Rabbi," Hanrahan said when they were back on the street.

They both knew what their next stop was. They moved toward their car parked in front of a fire hydrant. A handful of people were standing in the street watching nothing but knowing something was going on.

"What's goin' on?" asked an old woman, her coat pulled tight around her.

The two policemen didn't answer.

"I got a right," said the old woman. "Someone get killed or robbed or what? I got a right. I live right over there."

"You see anything last night, anyone going in that door?" asked Lieberman.

"No, besides, it's none of my business," she said defensively.

"I rest my case," said Lieberman, getting into the driver's seat while his partner rounded the car and got in.

They pulled into light traffic, past the car Wychovski had stolen the night before, went to the next corner, and turned right. The car with tinted windows that had been following them pulled out behind them and followed a half block behind.

When they got to North Avenue they turned right, went a few blocks, and parked. They locked up and walked half a block to the bingo parlor. The windows of the parlor were plastered with signs in Spanish, and a young man who

stood near the door stepped in front of them. Lieberman
didn't recognize him.

"*¿Donde esta El Chuculo?*" asked Lieberman.

"*¿Que quieres?*" asked the young man, looking from man
to man, one hand in his pocket.

"*Queremos hablar con Emiliano,*" said Lieberman.

"*No es posible. El esta ocupado.*"

"*Es necesario,*" said Lieberman.

"*No puedo hacerlo,*" said the determined young man.

Hanrahan suddenly reached out and grabbed the hand
the young man had in his pocket. The young man struggled, but Hanrahan held him tightly.

"Rabbi, tell him if he shoots, he'll blow his balls off,"
said Hanrahan.

"He knows," said Lieberman. "He may be more afraid
of El Perro than becoming a eunuch."

"*Soy El Viejo. Emiliano es mi amigo,*" said Lieberman.

"*¿Es verdad?*" asked the young man, his eyes fixed on
Hanrahan's with hate.

"*Sí. ¿Que es su nombre?*"

"Esteban."

"*Abre la puerta,* Esteban. *Tengo que hablar con Emiliano
cerca de Sammy Sosa.*"

Esteban really had no choice. Lieberman was giving the
new man in the Tentaculos a little wiggle room.

"Okay," Esteban said. "Let me go in and have someone
tell him you're here."

There was only the slightest touch of an accent to his
English.

"We don't know what's in your pocket, Esteban, and
right now we don't want to find out," said Lieberman. "I
just want to talk baseball with an old friend."

Esteban nodded and gave Hanrahan a cold you-haven't-seen-the-last-of-me look. Then he went inside and called someone's name.

"You've made a friend for life, Father Murphy."

"I try to spread goodwill wherever I tread, Rabbi."

Esteban was back almost instantly. He said nothing. Lieberman began counting to himself. When he got to ten, he was going in with or without the permission of Ghengis Del Sol. When he reached eight, the door opened and the two cops saw a face and body they recognized.

His name was Piedras, Stone. He was a block of brown granite with a flat face. Piedras was even bigger than Hanrahan. He was also extremely stupid and loyal to El Perro. He knew nothing, derived no meaning in life but through that loyalty and a passion for amazing quantities of food.

"*Buenos dias, Piedras*," said Lieberman.

"*Dias*," answered Piedras.

"*¿Esta Emiliano dentro del edificio?*"

"*Venga*," said Piedras, turning and entering the building.

The policemen followed him.

They moved through the inside doors and into the bingo parlor. Folding chairs and tables were missing, stored away. It looked like a dance floor.

"*Viejo*," called El Perro from the platform where he stood behind the table on which rested the steel-barred bingo machine.

El Perro was lean and smiling, apparently genuinely glad to see the older policeman. He ran one finger over the white scar on his face and opened his palm to look at a white bingo ball.

"Come on up," he said. "You too, Irish. Cubs are gonna be rained out today. They said. We can't go. And tonight . . ." He motioned around the empty room. "Tonight there's gonna be a dance here, for the church. We're gonna raise money to fix the walls."

"You're a saint," said Hanrahan.

"Fuckin' A right," said El Perro.

He wore black chinos and a white T-shirt.

"You see this ball?" he asked, holding up the ball in his hand. "I've been thinking. It's the only ball that's also a name, B4. That makes it special. Before. You know what I mean, *Viejo?*"

"B9," said Hanrahan.

"Huh?"

"Benign," Hanrahan repeated.

"What are you talkin' about? That's no fuckin' word."

"We've got a few questions, Emiliano."

Piedras stood behind the two policeman along with another member of the Tentaculos whom Lieberman recognized but whose name escaped him.

"B9," said El Perro. "You're a little loco like me, Irish."

"Arnold Sokol," said Lieberman.

"Are no so gal?" asked El Perro. "What the hell kind of question is that? Are no so gal? *¿Diga en Espanol?*"

"It's the same in Spanish," said Lieberman. "A name. Arnold Sokol." He said the name slowly.

"You want us to do something to this guy? Write his name. Tell me what you want. It's done. For you, *Viejo,* anything. You got *cojones.* That night you put the gun down Crazy Juan's pants in the Border Bar. Man, you were crazy. Place full of his friends. You all alone. Walked him right out. Didn't give a shit. He tried to run, and you shot in him the foot. Took two toes. I like you, *Viejo*, like a second father."

"I couldn't be more pleased," said Lieberman. "Arnold Sokol. He borrowed money from you, lots of money."

"I don't know this guy, Sokol," said El Perro. "You got me mixed up with some other Del Sol."

"He wrote your name in his appointment book," said Hanrahan. "El Perro."

"He wrote 'the dog' in his appointment book, and it's me? Bullshit, Irish."

El Perro laughed. Piedras stood stone-faced. The other Tentaculo smiled, afraid to laugh, afraid not to.

"You wouldn't lie to me would you, Emiliano?" asked Lieberman.

"Fuckin' A. Sure I'd lie to you. I lied to you a thousand times, but I got no reason to lie. I don' know this guy. I never loaned him no money."

"And you didn't kill him," Lieberman said.

"No. Not me. No Tentaculos. I never heard of this guy. Listen, *Viejo*, I'm having a very bad day. No baseball. No bingo. I think I'm coming down with something you know? Like a bug? Something. So don't hack me no Chinese."

Lieberman laughed.

"What's so funny?" Hanrahan.

"You mean don't '*hock me a chinek*,' " said Lieberman.

El Perro shrugged. He had picked up the Yiddish phrase from Lieberman, asked him what it meant, stored it away. Lieberman imagined him saying it to Piedras and wondered what other Yiddishisms the mad gang leader had picked up from him.

"Whatever," said El Perro. "I don't know this guy Sokol. *Cree o no?*"

"*Creo*, I believe you," said Lieberman. "You might want to check around and see if someone is using your name and reputation to loan shark."

"I'll check," said El Perro. "But they would have to be crazy to do it. Almost as crazy as I am."

Lieberman and Hanrahan turned and started to leave.

"What about next Saturday?" called El Perro. "Pittsburgh Pirates. Day game."

"I'll let you know," said Lieberman. "If I'm there, I'm there."

"Okay. *Adios*, B9," El Perro called.

On the street they moved past Esteban, who gave Hanrahan his best frightening look. Hanrahan paid no attention.

"You believe him, Rabbi?"

"Yeah, you?"

"I think so. So, someone's using his name and reputation," said Hanrahan.

"Someone's doing something."

"Like killing Arnold Sokol maybe?"

"Like killing Arnold Sokol maybe, Father Murphy. Let's check out our other suspects."

"Other business first," said Hanrahan. "What do you say you drive over to the guy who's been on our tail."

Lieberman saw the car. He knew what to do. He got in their car and started the engine while Hanrahan moved slowly around as if he were about to get in the passenger seat. Before Hanrahan reached the door, Lieberman hit the pedal, burned tire, and cut in front of a slow-moving battered pickup truck. He pulled alongside the car with tinted windows, blocking it in the space between the car ahead and the one behind.

The pickup truck driver cursed and slowed down as Hanrahan ran, pain surging through his knees, weapon in hand, to the sidewalk beyond the trapped car. Lieberman was out on the street now, his gun out and leveled in both hands at the driver's door.

"Open it up," Lieberman commanded.

There was a pause, and the window on the driver's side slid down slowly. Hanrahan moved to the front of the car, weapon pointed, then to the driver's side.

The man behind the wheel was familiar. Hanrahan had seen him four times before, and Lieberman had seen him twice. He was calm, wore sunglasses, and was definitely Chinese.

He was one of Laio Woo's personal bodyguards.

"Out of the car," Hanrahan commanded, coming to the open window and aiming his weapon.

The man behind the wheel sat calmly, his hands on the steering wheel. He reached up slowly to adjust his sunglasses and opened the door.

Hanrahan was on one side of him, Lieberman on the other.

The man who emerged from the car was slim and wore a navy blue Armani suit and red tie. He stood next to the open door, hands at his sides. Hanrahan reached over and patted him down. He was unarmed.

"You may not search my automobile," he said in clear, precise English. "I've committed no crime. My vehicle is properly registered, and my driver's license and license plates are current. You have no cause for invading my property."

"You were driving recklessly," said Lieberman. "Weaving in and out of traffic."

The man, who could not have been more than thirty, nodded in understanding and stepped toward Lieberman.

"There is a gun in my glove compartment," he said calmly. "Along with a license to carry it. My employer deals in very rare antiques and jewelry."

"Driver's license," said Lieberman.

The man slowly reached into his inner jacket pocket, produced a black leather wallet, and handed it to Lieberman.

Hanrahan slid past the man into the driver's seat. It was a tough squeeze but he managed to reach across and open the glove compartment.

"A Luger," he called back. "And registration with a permit to carry."

"There is nothing else of possible interest to you in my car," the young man said, "but if you wish to waste your time . . ."

Hanrahan came out of the car and slammed the door, almost catching the young man's right arm.

"What the hell are you doing? Why are you following me?" Hanrahan said evenly.

"I am your conscience," the young man said without a smile. "You promised Mr. Woo that you would not marry Miss Chen for one year, that you would consider the reasons why this might not be a good or proper union. There are still eight months to go on your promise."

"I promised nothing," said Hanrahan.

"That is not Mr. Woo's interpretation of the situation," the young man said. "Nor that of Miss Chen's father. And it is Mr. Woo's understanding that you intend to marry precipitously."

A small crowd had gathered on the sidewalk and in the street where Lieberman had parked. All of the faces were Hispanic. Behind him Lieberman heard the voice of El Perro.

"What's goin' on?" he said. "What's this Korean gook doin'?"

Lieberman's cell phone began to buzz.

"He's Chinese," said Lieberman.

"Same difference," said El Perro, looking at Mr. Woo's man, who turned his tinted glasses toward the gang leader with a look of complete disinterest. "What's he doin' here?"

"He's a bad driver," said Lieberman. "*No puede manajar un automóvil muy bien.*"

The phone kept buzzing.

"*No lo creo. ¿Dígame, Viejo, que pasa?*"

"This gentleman," Lieberman said, looking at the driver's license in the wallet, "Mr. Ye, is being given a warning for reckless driving. Mr. Ye is now being told that if we see him driving recklessly, which means if we see him driving, we will be forced to arrest him for a variety of infractions. Which means we don't want to see Mr. Ye anymore."

He handed the wallet back to Ye, who returned it to his pocket. Lieberman answered the phone.

"Lieberman."

"Abe, you know what time it is?" came Bess's voice.

He looked at his watch. It was a few minutes past noon.

"You're supposed to be at the temple for the fund-raiser

lunch meeting," Bess said wearily. "Did you eat this morning? Did you get any sleep?"

"You're up to something, *Viejo*," said El Perro. "Pull away and don't look back. You know, I think our Chink here is going to have an accident. I think our Chink here is maybe not gonna live, and if he does, he's gonna know what part of the city to stay out of."

"I ate oatmeal at Maish's," Lieberman told Bess. "I caught a few hours in the car. I shaved at the station, put on fresh underwear and a shirt from my locker. Bess, I'm kind of busy right now."

"Filth," said Ye, looking at El Perro, then away.

"What?" shouted El Perro. "What'd he call me?"

"I didn't hear," said Lieberman. "Mr. Ye, I suggest you get back in your car. I'll back up and let you out, and we'll watch you drive away."

"What's going on, Abe?" Bess asked.

"I'm busy. I can't make the luncheon. Go in my place."

"Where do you think I am? I'm at the luncheon."

"Then tell everyone I'm sorry. There's been a death in the family. The family of man. Ask Rabbi Wass if he's seen the news about Arnold Sokol. He'll understand."

"Abe, you told them you would be there," Bess said firmly.

"Okay, I'll get there as soon as I can. Half an hour."

Lieberman hung up and pocketed the phone.

"Tell Woo if he wants to see me," Hanrahan was saying to Ye, "he knows where I live, and he has my number. I don't like mind games."

Ye got in his car and turned to look at El Perro.

"What is the word your people are called? Spics?"

"You are dead sushi," screamed El Perro, now being held back by Hanrahan and Lieberman.

"The Japanese eat sushi not the Chinese, you racist spic."

"I've got your fuckin' license number," El Perro screamed. "You disrespect me in front of my people." He spread his arms, indicating the crowd. "I'm gonna find you and cut your *pequeño* yellow dick off."

Ye shook his head.

"I'm gonna kill him, *Viejo*. You didn' hear me say it, remember, but I'm gonna kill him."

"You'll have to go to Chinatown to do it, Emiliano," said Lieberman. "He works for Woo."

"I give no shit about that Chinese gang, tong shit," said El Perro, the white scar on his face pulsing. "I'll go in there alone."

"Cubs. Saturday," Lieberman said.

"He's dead, *Viejo*."

"Lieber's pitching, I think," said Lieberman. "I'll see you at Wrigley."

Hanrahan held El Perro back while Lieberman went back to the car and backed up so Ye could get out. Ye seemed to be in no hurry.

The street was full of people now, all looking at El Perro, knowing who he was. Tentaculos surrounded their leader. Someone was going to suffer and soon. If it wasn't going to be the Chinese guy, it might be someone on the street who made the mistake of looking at El Perro too long or the wrong way. The crowd began to disperse.

When Ye was out of sight heading toward Michigan Avenue, Hanrahan got in the car and Lieberman drove away looking into his rearview mirror. He could see El Perro looking around, fists clenched in rage. He didn't want to see more.

"Congratulations, Father Murphy. It looks like you've started an unusual if not unique gang war. Latinos and Chinese. They don't even have a border or business dispute. Just reputation."

"Reputation means everything," Hanrahan said, looking straight forward.

Lieberman wasn't sure if his partner was talking about the Chinese, the Tentaculos, both, or himself.

Z and Eddie got to Jamie's one-room basement apartment in a wooden frame house on Kimball at around eleven. Z wasn't feeling too well. Actually, he felt like shit. His head hurt, hurt like hell. Little shocks on top of a constant pressure and ache in his head. The rest of him didn't feel that great either.

Sokol was dead. Good. Jamie killed him. Let's give him a medal, Z thought as he led the way down the five steps to Jamie's apartment. No, let the cops give him the prize.

"Good job," Z would say. "Thanks for doing the bastard. You should have driven a truck over him. Sorry Eddie and I had to give you up, but hey, what can you do? Cops are after us, and we're clean. Cops are going to come after you soon, and you are stupid.

Z knocked at the door.

"Who's it?" called Jamie.

"Z and Eddie."

The door opened. Jamie stood there in his jeans. No shirt, no socks or shoes. He was the biggest of the trio, the strongest, the dumbest. His hair was blond, cut short, and an island of fine yellow hair nested on his chest. His mouth was open, and he looked at Z.

"You okay?" he asked, stepping out of the way.

"Do I look okay?" asked Z, stepping in with Eddie behind him.

"You look . . . I don' know. Not so good I guess."

The room was neat. Jamie hated dirt and was afraid of roaches, rats, spiders, anything that crawled. He had nightmares about a roach crawling on his chest. Jamie kept cans of bug spray and scrubbed the room almost every day. He kept the sheets, blanket, and pillowcases on his bed in the middle of the room clean. He didn't want to sleep against a wall. Something might crawl up or down the wall, and if there were rats, and there almost certainly were in the old building, he would hear them.

Whenever he spent time at Eddie's trailer, the first thing he did when he got back to the apartment was throw all his clothes in the washing machine, including his sneakers, then take a long hot shower.

"I was doing laundry," he said, as Z moved to the park bench against the wall. The bench had been stolen from a park in DesPlaines. Jamie used it as a couch. Two pillows, plain brown, which he had dry-cleaned every month. There was a small wooden table with three chairs, an ancient electric range against one wall, with a noisy refrigerator next to it, and a dresser in a corner of the room with a big-screen color television sitting on it.

There was a soccer game going on on TV. The sound was off.

"It's in Italian or something," said Jamie nervously, moving to turn off the television. "I can't understand Italian."

"I know," said Z.

Eddie moved to the refrigerator and opened it. He knew he wouldn't find anything he wanted to eat, but there might be a Coke or something. There wasn't.

Z sat on the sofa bench and looked at Jamie, who stood in front of him. Eddie went to sit on one of the wooden chairs by the table.

"So," Jamie said. "You're okay."

"I told you."

"Yeah, that's right. You did. You're not okay."

Jamie rubbed his pants nervously against his sides.

"So he's dead. That guy who . . . the other night," Jamie went on.

"He's dead."

"It was on television," Jamie said. "Guy's name. Stuff."

"Yeah, thanks," said Z. "You got any aspirin, anything?"

"Motrin?"

"Yeah."

"Why did you say 'thanks'?" Jamie said, moving to the cabinet next to the refrigerator. He opened the door. Everything was laid out neatly. Every box that had been opened was in a sealed see-through bag.

"For doing Sokol," said Z. "For getting back for me."

"And me, too," Eddie added.

Jamie had the Motrin now. He brought the bottle to Z, who opened it, poured about five of them into his hand, and threw them into his mouth. For years he had been able to take only one pill at a time and with lots of water. A year or so ago he found that he could suddenly swallow pills without water, just gulp them down. He couldn't figure, but who cared. Right now he didn't care about anything but a confession from Jamie.

"So, thanks," Z said.

"You're welcome," said Jamie.

"Yeah, thanks," Eddie added again.

Jamie turned his head to look at him and nodded with a smile.

"Where'd you find him?" Z asked.

"Find him?"

"The guy. You killed him for all of us," said Z. "Right?"

"The dead guy?"

Jamie was looking at Z and trying to think. Z smiled, a smile that looked like gratitude and respect.

"So," said Z. "How'd you find him? I mean before you killed him?"

"Over by the rocks," said Jamie slowly. "He went back there. I went back there."

"Why?" asked Eddie.

"Why?" Jamie repeated. "To look for something I dropped."

"What?" asked Z.

"My watch. He was there. I beat the shit out of him and pushed him in the water. He hit his face on the rocks."

"You didn't mean to kill him?" asked Z.

"Just rough him, hurt him, for you," Jamie said.

"Cops are gonna come," said Z. "You better make up a story."

Jamie stood running his tongue back and forth over his lower lip.

"I was with you, you and Eddie at the hospital. You'll back me. Same story. With you all night."

"Should work," said Z, standing up, feeling no better. "I'm going over to Eddie's for the night."

"Okay," said Jamie. "We getting together later?"

"Depends on how I feel," said Z. "We'll call. Let's go, Eddie."

"See you, Jamie," said Eddie, following Z to the door. "Thanks again."

"See you," said Jamie.

Out on the sidewalk heading toward the car Z said, "Cops want us all."

"Yeah," said Eddie.

"You and I didn't do anything."

"No."

"So, we give them Jamie," said Z.

Eddie went to the driver's side and got in. When they were both inside, doors closed, Eddie said, "We give 'em Jamie."

"Can't wait for police," Wychovski said, grabbing the woman's arm.

She turned to face him. She knew. He could see she knew. Not the details. Not even a general idea of what was inside the circle he was trapped in. But she knew the outline. She had seen people there, maybe been there herself.

"Man trying to kill you, man with a shotgun. There's no place you can walk or run around here. You're a white man. Try looking in the mirror sometime."

Wychovski didn't want to look in a mirror. He didn't want to run.

"Somebody you can call?" she asked.

"No. I can boost a car."

"Nothing you find on the streets around here," she said. "People lock their cars up in garages if they got 'em, or keep an eye on 'em. You see a lot of cars parked out there?"

Wychovski remembered seeing cars. Not a lot but some.

"Go try and steal a car. You'll have a whole gang of black faces coming for you. You kill someone? Wait. Don't answer that. There's a door back down this hall, leads to the basement. There's a table and a chair near the furnace. Just sit there till it gets dark. I've got my son's sweatshirt with a hood in the dryer, along with his other stuff. Yours has blood on it. My sons'll fit you. Put it on and wait. I'm gonna be late for work."

"Here," said Wychovski, reaching into his pocket and taking out a golden turtle. "It's real."

She took it, turned it over, and put it in her pocket.

"Be gone from here when it turns first dark. Hear what I'm sayin'."

"I hear," he said.

The woman nodded and went back out the front door without looking back. He moved to the window, parted the curtain, and watched her walk down the stairs and across the street.

She was going to sell him out. He was sure. Why shouldn't she? Dickerson was roaming. She might find him if she were dishonest enough. Or she could find a phone and call the cops. Either way he wasn't going down into the cellar. He would take his chances in the street. This was a big goddamn city, the toddling town. Big, bad, millions of people. Head east down the alleys. Head toward downtown, toward State Street. That great street. Find a car. Take a chance. Get the hell out of the city.

He still had some of the watches. He still had golden animals left. How many people were dead? He fingered something hard in his pocket, wondering what it was. A tiger? How many were dead? Pryor. The cop. Walter. Three.

The street looked clear. Near the corner three girls, teens, maybe a little older, were standing. They looked as if they were waiting for a ride.

He could feel the pulse in his forehead. He could feel, really feel, his heart beating. He stepped through the door and heard the voices of the girls on the corner though he couldn't make out what they were saying.

Dickerson had gone west. Wychovski went down the steps and moved east, toward downtown. Don't run. Don't hurry. No, he had to hurry. And what was the difference if he ran. Dickerson would recognize him two blocks away.

He jogged, looking down each street as he came to a corner. Avoiding the eyes of the few people he passed. He wanted rain. It looked as if it were going to rain. Rain would bring daylight darkness. Rain would discourage Dickerson. Well, it might. Dickerson had the money, but he wasn't safe. He needed Wychovski, and he needed him dead.

As he moved faster, he considered things he could have been and done. He could have been a good salesman. He could have been a dealer in Atlantic City or on some Indian reservation. He looked as if he might have some Indian blood in him. He could make it up. He would be a good dealer. Used cars. New cars. He could sell them. He could fix them. He could drive them.

He had been in Daytona once. The noise from the track was deafening. If the noise were here and it had been blackness instead of thick sound, he could hide.

Hungry. He hadn't considered it. He was hungry. He was probably also tired, but he didn't feel tired.

Bring it together. Boost a car. Get to another car outside

the city. Boost it. Make his way to St. Louis, where he had money.

Now he had a plan. It was good to have a plan, to work out the details as he moved. He had been walking about ten minutes when he heard the siren. He couldn't tell where the sound was coming from. He moved down the street to his left. A big street. Dickerson might think twice with cops around. Might think twice about walking around with a shotgun and a suitcase full of money.

Wychovski found himself on Van Buren Street. The cop car was coming down the street toward him. He pulled the hood over his face, put his hands in his pockets, moved to the nearest store, and went in. Through the window of the neighborhood grocery no more than the size of a two-car garage, he watched the cops.

"Car crashed down the street," a man's voice called out. "Big new car. Brother came out with a gun shooting at a white ma . . ."

The man had been in the back of the store putting something on a shelf. Now he spotted Wychovski and knew from his eyes who he was looking at.

Wychovski held up both hands, palms out to show they were empty. He put his right hand back in his pocket and came up with a woman's watch with a gold-and-diamond band. He also came up with a golden parrot.

He put them both on the small cluttered counter, looked into the eyes of the old man and shook his head no. The old man shook his head no in return, and Wychovski went out the door and back to the street.

Thunder now. It was definitely going to rain. He walked quickly for half a block, and the rain began. People were running for cover. He ran too, ran east, ran fast. His pock-

ets jingled with what remained of the disaster he and Pryor
had created.

What was there in man that sought out punishment for
imagined misdeeds? Lieberman wondered. Well, actually,
Lieberman had to admit that some of his own misdeeds
were not imagined.

He sat in Rabbi Wass's study pretending to listen to Irving Trammel. Irving was a lawyer, not yet forty, well
dressed, fully suited, even had a pocket watch. His dark
hair was brushed straight back and he was lecturing.

It was a dour group. Rabbi Wass, seated behind his desk,
didn't seem to be listening, though his unfocused eyes were
aimed at the man Lieberman unaffectionately called Erwin
Rommel. Lieberman was sure the Rabbi's mind was on the
death of Arnold Sokol. Ida Katzman, who was moving in
fast on her eighty-eighth birthday, sat in the chair next to
Lieberman, leaning on her cane. Ida Katzman could not
shrink much more and still exist. She did not bother to
look at Irving Trammel. Her eyes were on Lieberman. Ida
Katzman didn't have to pretend to look at Irving. She was
ancient and rich, both of which gave her the advantage of
not having to pretend to deal with people she didn't like.
She didn't like Trammel, Abe knew, but Irving knew what
he was doing. The ancient woman was the financial core
of the congregation. The lawyer was the corporate center,
and the rabbi the reminder that the temple existed for spir-
itual reasons.

Syd Levan was the only one paying attention to Irving.
Syd was Lieberman's age, owner of two children's furniture
stores in the suburbs. He wasn't rich. He wasn't poor. He
kept in reasonable shape, had great false teeth and a win-

ning smile. His hair was a well-dyed black, and he felt truly honored to be in the inner circle.

Lieberman had dropped Bill Hanrahan at the station, and they agreed Bill would pick up his partner at Lieberman's house at two-fifteen. That gave Lieberman time to make an appearance at the meeting and an excuse to leave it within an hour. Bill said he had some things to take care of, too. Abe hadn't asked what they were.

"So," the Desert Fox continued, or, Lieberman hoped, concluded, "if we can get a really big-name speaker, we can charge one-fifty a plate and make a profit of $15,000 if we sell all the tickets."

"Providing we don't have to pay the speaker," said Lieberman.

"We can pay four thousand and still make fifteen," said Trammel with a knowing smile. "I've worked the numbers. If we get a big enough name, we can get the bigger dining room at the Hyatt. We pay three thousand more and it is not beyond the realm of real possibility that we could make $30,000 or more."

He had someone in mind. They all knew it, but only Syd seemed the least curious.

"Who?" he asked.

"Lieberman," said the Desert Fox.

Everyone looked at Abe.

"No," Trammel corrected, "Joseph Lieberman. We give him an award, let him name the date."

"We just call his office and ask him?" asked Syd.

"Abe calls his office and asks him," said Trammel. "One Lieberman to another. Maybe you're distant cousins."

"I see a family resemblance," said Syd, studying Abe.

"I defer to the orator," Abe said, looking at Trammel.

Trammel wouldn't take up the ball. He would just pass it. He would not want to come up with the idea and then fail to have it succeed. Far better to come up with the idea and let Abe fail.

"I respectfully decline," said the Fox. "Syd and I are already taking on the dinner. I checked with the temple president about this before I proposed it."

The temple president was Abe's wife, Bess.

"When?"

"An hour ago," Irving said, now a step ahead in the chess game of responsibility.

Abe looked to the rabbi for help. There was none there. He looked at Ida Katzman. She could reach into her little beaded purse, pull out her checkbook, and write a check for $30,000. She had done it many times before, but there was a limit to the number of times the committee could go to Ida. The library was named for her long-deceased husband. The building carried a bronze plaque thanking her for making the move to the new temple a reality. From Bess, Abe knew that the old woman had donated more than two million dollars to the temple over the ten years since her husband's death.

"Because I have the same name as the senator? That's a reason?"

"Why not?" asked Syd.

"And you're a police officer," Irving added. "You're more likely to get through to him."

Abe looked at Ida, who shrugged. He couldn't tell what the shrug meant. He hoped it meant that she would not cast the vote her money gave her to make him do it. It might also mean she sided with Syd's "why not." And then again she might simply have felt a chill.

Everyone was looking at Abe, who reached up to run a finger along his gray mustache, a sign Bess would recognize. Abe Lieberman was trapped.

"I didn't even vote for him," Abe confessed.

"You voted for Bush?" Rabbi Wass said, jolted to life.

"I voted Libertarian," said Lieberman. "Now you know my politics. An open book."

"And Bess . . . ?" Ida Katzman said, now paying attention.

"She voted Democratic," said Abe. "It's in her genes. You don't want me to make this call."

"We do," Ida Katzman said.

That ended the conversation.

"I'll call," Abe said with unconcealed resignation. "No promises. I'll call his office."

"I have his office number," said Trammel, reaching into his pocket and pulling out his wallet.

"Why does that not surprise me?" Lieberman asked, as the lawyer handed him a card. It was Irving's business card. On the back was the name: Senator Joseph Lieberman. There was a telephone number, an e-mail address, and a fax number.

"You can call today," said Irving.

Lieberman pocketed the card.

"I've got a couple of murderers to find today. I'll call in the morning," said Abe.

"Then," said Trammel with a small but triumphant smile, "I have no other items on the agenda."

"Then we're finished," said Rabbi Wass.

Lieberman knew that he was. He was suddenly very, very hungry. If he were lucky, Bess would be home. If he were lucky, there would still be some of last night's dessert in the refrigerator. If he were lucky, he could get her to call Joe Lieberman's office. It would cost him something. Bess would have a price, but Abe would probably be willing to pay it.

"You play golf, Abe?" Syd Levan asked, as Trammel moved quickly to talk to Ida Katzman and help her up.

"No, Syd. How long have you known me?"

"Thirty, forty years," said Levan, showing his expensive teeth.

"Have I ever played golf with you?"

"No, but it doesn't hurt to ask."

"I don't play golf, Syd. I do drink coffee, and on rare occasions I eat. You want to get together for lunch at the T&L sometime and kibbitz, I'm open."

Syd had lost his wife to cancer about a year ago. It had been sudden, unexpected. Syd had seemed to recover quickly, to handle it well. He threw himself into his work along with his two daughters and sons-in-law. He joined temple committees, and he developed a passion for golf, which, Lieberman had heard, he played well.

"Lunch sounds good," said Syd. "You really have two killers to find today?"

"If possible," said Abe, looking at the forlorn rabbi, who was moving around the desk slowly to say his good-byes.

"Gotta talk to Irving," Syd said, touching Lieberman's arm and moving to flank Ida Katzman and help her out the door.

"Abraham," Rabbi Wass called, as Lieberman moved toward the door behind the slowly departing trio, "you have a minute?"

Lieberman turned, and Rabbi Wass moved forward, hesitating till the other three committee members were gone.

Rabbi Wass looked about five years older and ten pounds heavier than he had the day before. He was wearing a clean white shirt and dark trousers and the usual black yarmulke on his head. He also wore the look of a troubled man.

"Arnold Sokol, the man in the hospital, was murdered?" asked the Rabbi softly.

"Yes," said Lieberman.

"Did the young man at the hospital, Zembinsky, is there a chance he killed Mr. Sokol?"

Lieberman thought he knew where this was going.

"It's a possibility," said Lieberman. "We're working on it."

"So," said the rabbi, adjusting his glasses, "I may have kept Arnold Sokol from killing Melvin Zembinsky in the hospital, but Melvin Zembinsky may then have murdered Arnold Sokol?"

Lieberman stood waiting till the rabbi went on.

"It's a difficult question. Was I destined by God to be a part of this human . . ."

"Joke?" Lieberman supplied.

"No, 'puzzle' perhaps. Is one life worth more than another? And why was I the instrument of this . . . I'm sorry, just thinking aloud. I've learned to accept the will of the almighty even when I don't understand it."

"And my brother has learned to reject the will of the Almighty when he doesn't understand it," Lieberman said.

"God has a sardonic sense of irony," said the rabbi with a shake of his head. "There's a sermon in all of this somewhere, but I don't know where. I'll work on it. Please let me know if Melvin Zembinsky was in any way responsible for the murder of Mr. Sokol."

"I'll let you know," said Lieberman, who had no intention of thinking about divine nonintervention in the affairs of man.

Things simply were, Lieberman had long ago concluded. Read the Torah, and that's the lesson you get. At least that was the lesson Lieberman got. Don't look for reasons, for why bad things happen to good people or good things to bad people. The first five books of the Scriptures are filled with God's playing favorites, playing tricks, playing games, manipulating for no other reason than that's the way he feels like doing it. Therein, Lieberman had decided, lay the lesson. Learn to accept whatever happens, to be ready for anything if you can, and to blame not God but man or chance or God's whim. Sometimes Lieberman felt that there was no such thing as a simple God, but there were very wise people who wrote the Torah and put in the simple message: Don't try to understand or explain. Simply accept that anything can happen.

Lieberman's thinking, however, had gone a step further. If God wasn't going to do anything when bad things happened to good people, and if the law didn't take care of the problem, Abraham Lieberman was willing to take on the responsibility. He would discuss his actions with God if and when that opportunity arose.

There were only a few cars parked on Lieberman's street. One of the cars was Bill Hanrahan's. Abe parked in front of his partner's car, moved across the lawn and up the three concrete steps to his front door. He could hear his wife talking when he opened the door.

He stepped in and saw her sitting next to Hanrahan.

"Joseph Lieberman," Abe said when he had closed the door.

"Will it hurt you to call?" said Bess.

She was wearing her red suit. She had somewhere to go or had just come back. Abe liked her in red. He was in a red mood.

"You call. I'll clean the garage. Fair exchange."

He walked into the dining room and sat across the table from his wife and partner.

"Abe," she said with a sigh. "What's the worst that could happen? He could say 'no.' "

Abe was about to further his protest, but he looked at his partner. Hanrahan clearly had something on his mind. His big fingers were playing with his coffee cup. A small pool of coffee sat in the saucer.

"What?" Lieberman asked.

"Bill and Iris want to get married."

"I know."

"Tomorrow," said Bess. "They've got the license. That Unitarian minister will marry them. They want us to be there."

"Tomorrow," Lieberman repeated.

Hanrahan nodded.

"Iris agreed. Later we'll have a celebration or something for our relatives, friends. Woo isn't going to give up. When it's done, over, he'll have to accept that what's done is done."

"And if he doesn't?" asked Lieberman.

"What's he going to do? Kill the bridegroom? Iris isn't going to marry him, and he's too smart to try to kill me."

"I'm not sure 'smart' would have much to do with it," said Abe. "Maybe 'smart' is killing you and letting his people know that he's as dangerous to cross as they already know he is."

"Iris says she doesn't think so," said Hanrahan. "Rabbi, we're gonna do it. Bess says she's in."

"Then I'm in," said Lieberman. "Tomorrow I call Joe Lieberman and witness a wedding. On the side we can try to find a couple of killers. Congratulations and good luck."

"We might need it," said Hanrahan, taking his partner's hand.

"Now," said Lieberman. "What do we say to a small repast?"

"I called Kearney. They picked up Zembinsky and his two friends. They weren't hiding. Got 'em waiting for us at the station."

"Then we'll eat fast, and they can have a little time to contemplate their sinful ways."

"Amen," said Hanrahan.

"Lox omelettes," said Bess. "With or without onions?"

"With," said Lieberman.

"Definitely 'with,' " echoed Hanrahan.

"And cream cheese," said Lieberman as Bess rose.

She gave him a reproachful look and a shaking of her head.

"Just a little," Lieberman said. "It won't kill me. And whatever that secret dessert from last night was if there's any left."

Bess went into the kitchen. He had no idea if she would return with cream cheese in the omelettes and a dessert.

The thin black woman in her fifties sat back straight, both feet firmly on the worn wooden floor of the Clark Street Station squad room. She wore a brown dress and carried a tan cloth bag, which she clutched to her almost nonexistent breasts.

The flabby white man who was probably less than forty sat rocking forward and back, both legs vibrating from side to side. The flabby man who was either trying to grow a beard or simply hadn't shaved in a few days was making a hissing sound through his teeth as he rocked.

Wedged between the thin woman and the flabby man on the narrow wooden bench was Eddie Denenberg, who wanted to move away from both of them but had no place to go. When he tried to get up, the detective at the desk about a dozen feet in front of him motioned for him to sit back down.

The detective's name was Rodriguez. It said so in white on the black plaque on his desk. He looked like a Rodriguez to Eddie, dark, tough, and not in a good mood.

Rodriguez was talking to a girl no more than sixteen,

who sat in the chair next to his desk. She talked quietly and earnestly, using her hands a lot. The girl wore a short skirt and a halter top and kept brushing back her long, straight hair. Rodriguez listened to her and kept an eye on Eddie as Lieberman had asked him.

Eddie pointed to his crotch and squirmed, doing his mime of a man in urgent need of a toilet. Rodriguez didn't care. Eddie sat. The thin black woman kept looking straight ahead. The flabby man kept rocking.

The squad room was busy, very busy. Every desk had a detective behind it. Noise, voices, someone belched, someone cried, more than one voice was raised in indignation and anger. All the cops seemed to wear the same look, weary, resigned. Not angry, not unsympathetic, just resigned.

They had all been picked up together, Eddie, Z, and Jamie at Eddie's trailer. The cops who came just asked them to show ID, told them not to talk, and took them away in a patrol car.

When they got to the station, they sat Eddie on the bench and took Z and Jamie away. Z had gone over it with him before Jamie had come to the trailer.

"Tell 'em nothing," Z had said. "They ask. You say nothing. They tell you me or Jamie talked, you make a deal, you hold out, and when they threaten you with all kinds of bullshit, tell them you'll give 'em what they want if they let you walk. Then you tell them what Jamie said about killing Sokol."

"The truth?"

"The truth," Z had said.

Now Eddie sat. The squad room door opened. A big

cop came in, looked toward Eddie, and motioned for him to follow. Eddie got up. The flabby man spread out to fill the void. The black woman inched farther toward the end of the bench.

The cop led him into the corridor where cops, perps, victims, and witnesses were being ushered in and out and up and down.

A short fat woman with her straight gray hair held back tight with a rubber band was being supported by a black policewoman.

The fat woman was saying, "I kin make it. I kin make it."

The big cop opened a door right across from the squad room. The fat woman pointed at Eddie, the flab under her upper arms shook.

"That him? That the bastard who cut up my Bonny?"

"No," said the policewoman. "Just come with me."

Eddie went into the room in front of the detective. The large room was almost empty. There were two unmatched folding chairs in the middle of the room. The floors had a fresh coat of something green that looked like concrete. One wall was painted green, and someone had stopped halfway through painting another wall. There were cans of paint on the floor and a large rolled-up drop cloth.

"Gonna be the new lockup," said the big cop. "Have a seat."

Eddie moved to one of the folding chairs and sat. The big cop sat in the other chair and said, "My name's Detective Hanrahan. I'm in a pretty good mood, but I'm Irish, and I'm not a patient man. You've got a little room to wiggle but not much. Now, let's talk."

In the interrogation room at the rear of the squad room, Lieberman sat on one side of the scarred, scratched, and stained wooden table. Melvin Zembinsky sat on the other side. There was a cup of Dunkin' Donuts coffee on the table in front of Zembinsky. Lieberman was drinking from a similar cup.

"I drink it with cream and sugar," said Zembinsky, leaning back and folding his arms.

"I've got some Equal."

"Forget it," said Zembinsky, reaching for the coffee and glancing at the mirror that covered most of the wall to his right. There were no windows in the room, but it was bright. A bank of eight fluorescents tinkled overhead.

Zembinsky knew that he was being watched by someone behind the mirror, maybe another cop or two, someone who could ID him for something, a prosecutor. He had an audience. Good. He'd play to them, have some fun before he turned Jamie over.

He was wrong. There was no one behind the mirror in the little observation room.

"You like oranges?" Lieberman asked.

"Sometimes. You offering me an orange?"

"No, just curious. You like baseball?"

"Sometimes."

"Cubs or Sox fan?"

"I don' know. You want to ask me something that makes fuckin' sense, then ask."

"You kill Arnold Sokol?"

"No," Z said, reaching for the coffee.

"You know who did?"

"No."

"I think you killed him. The man in the bed next to yours in the hospital said you got up during the night and were gone for a couple of hours."

"I was in the john reading *People* magazine," said Z. "Cover to cover. I like to keep up. I was in there half an hour, maybe less."

"You like Johnny Depp?"

"He's alright. What the hell has this . . . ?"

"I still think you killed him."

"You arresting me? Read me my rights and get me a lawyer."

"Your father? He's a lawyer, isn't he?"

Z put down the coffee carefully and very slowly said, "I don't want my father. It's a mutual kind of thing. I don't want him. He doesn't want me."

"It's good when a father and son don't want the same thing," said Lieberman. "I've got a daughter. We never want the same thing."

"She got a nice ass?" asked Z, with a glance at the mirror.

Lieberman shrugged.

"My daughter is too old and too tough for you," said Lieberman. "She'd have you pleading to murders you didn't commit just to get someplace safe. Might be a good idea. Turn my daughter loose on you for four hours. Just the two of you locked in a room talking."

"I didn't kill anyone. I don't think I'm gonna need a lawyer. I need some aspirin, maybe codeine."

Z let his right hand move to the bandage covering the section of shaved scalp in which he had a dozen stitches.

"Want me to take a look at your head?" Lieberman said with a smile.

This wasn't going the way Z expected. The little Jew cop was nuts.

"No. I didn't kill Sokol."

"Coincidence," said Lieberman. "One night you try to mug him, and he sends you to the hospital. A day later he's murdered, and you don't know anything about it. I think we've got you for all kinds of things if not murder. Attempted murder is a good one. Or we drop down to assault and attempted robbery. That's not really up to me."

"What happens if, and this is just an 'if,' if I know who killed Sokol?"

"We charge you with withholding evidence and maybe being an accomplice," said Lieberman. "Or maybe if you tell me everything and fast, you walk away, a good citizen. Maybe I recommend you for a medal. You go to City Hall, shake the mayor's hand, and he hangs a medal on a ribbon around your neck."

Lieberman sat back, drinking his coffee. He looked toward the mirror and nodded, though he knew no one was in the observation room.

Melvin Zembinsky had something to say. Lieberman knew it the second he had sat the young man in the chair. The game was to get Lieberman to push him into talking. At least that's what Zembinsky's game was. Lieberman's was to make Zembinsky squirm and talk.

"Let's talk a deal," said Zembinsky, leaning forward across the table.

"Let's talk Polish," said Lieberman. "Listen, I think you need a lawyer. I've got another case to work on. Just ask me for a lawyer. I'll put you in holding. Your lawyer will come and . . ."

"Jamie did it," Z said.

"James Franzen? Your coffee's getting cold."

Z drank some more coffee.

"I can stick it in the microwave for a minute," said Lieberman, reaching for the cup.

"Forget the fuckin' coffee. Jamie did it. He told me and Eddie this morning. We went to his place from the hospital. Ask Eddie."

"You told him to kill Sokol."

"Hell no."

"You willing to write out what Jamie told you and sign it?"

"Yeah."

"I'll get you a pen and paper. When you're done, you can read it into a tape recorder."

"Fine."

Lieberman looked at the mirror. So did Z. Z saw faint outlines of moving bodies where Lieberman knew there were none. Lieberman left the room to let Zembinsky work out his act.

The squad room did smell. No doubt. Only Cooper denied it. Cooper had no sense of smell. He thought all the other cops made up the business about the smell to fool around with him. Cooper didn't care. He had five years to go until retirement. Compared to what they pulled on Connie Faldo, squad room smell gags were a walk on the yellow brick road.

Hanrahan wasn't at his desk. A new detective, young, caved-in chest and bad skin, sat in Hanrahan's chair playing with his suspenders and shaking his head while two old men sat across from him imploring. Lieberman moved around desks and bodies, went into the corridor, where he saw Hanrahan standing at the window near the stairs, looking out at the rain.

"Yours?" asked Lieberman.

"Turned over his friend Franzen. Took all of ten minutes. Yours?"

"Beat you by three minutes."

"Get 'em on the jury. They'll vote to get the death penalty moving again. It's good to have friends, Rabbi."

"Good indeed," Lieberman agreed. "Time for Jamie."

"Time."

Melvin Zembinsky was moved to a desk in the squad room, where he could write his statement and be watched by Rodriguez. He could see Eddie five desks over doing the same thing. Their eyes met. Z nodded. Eddie nodded back. Jamie was history.

Jamie Franzen, golden-haired and in a clean blue T-shirt and jeans, stood in front of the same table in the interrogation room where Z had sat minutes before.

This time when Lieberman entered the room there was someone behind the mirror, Bill Hanrahan and Alan Kearney.

"Sit down," Lieberman said.

"I like standing," said Jamie.

"I'm already having a long day," said Lieberman wearily. "Make both of our lives easier."

"This place isn't clean," said Jamie. I heard something in the trash basket."

He looked at the wastebasket in the corner. The basket was full, topped by two Dunkin' Donuts coffee containers.

"You going to run if you see a roach come out of the can?" asked Lieberman.

"Maybe. What do you want?"

"Your best buddies, Melvin and Edward, say you told them this morning that you killed Arnold Sokol last night," said Lieberman.

Jamie stood blinking for a few seconds. He didn't glance at the mirror. All he saw was the little cop sitting across the table.

"What did you do to them?"

"Talked to them for about a minute or two," said Lieberman. "They couldn't wait to turn you in."

"You're lying."

"Got you nailed, James," said Lieberman with a shake of his head.

"Is prison dirty?" asked Jamie.

"No," said Lieberman. "It's pretty clean. They keep it that way. Plenty of time and Lysol and not enough to do. Now I can't vouch for the jail."

"Jail?"

"Cook County Jail till your trial," said Lieberman. "We'll see what we can do about getting you a place without roaches."

"Or ants, or spiders, rats, mice, beetles. They're so goddamn dirty," said Jamie. "You gotta work all the time to keep them out of everything."

"I know," said Lieberman. "You know you are now under arrest for the murder of Arnold Sokol. You have . . ."

"I know," Jamie said. "I don't want a lawyer. I want to tell you what happened. If Eddie and Z don't want to stand up for me, I'll show 'em I'll stand up for them."

"Because they're your buddies?" asked Lieberman.

"Because you stand up for your friends even if they don't stand up for you."

"Then tell me," said Lieberman.

Jamie Franzen pulled out the folding chair, examined it, then picked it up and turned it over to inspect the underside of the seat. Satisfied, he put the chair down and sat.

Franzen: Last night I went to his house.

Lieberman: Whose house?

Franzen: Sokol.

Lieberman: To kill him?

Franzen: Beat him to shit. Yeah, maybe kill him for what he did to me and Z.

Lieberman: How did you know where he lived?

Franzen: Phone book.

Lieberman: Were there any other Arthur Sokols in the phone book?

Franzen: No, I don't think so. I went there and called him from a pay phone, told him I had something of his, that all he had to do was come downstairs and get it.

Lieberman: And he came?

Franzen: No. He said he was going to call the police. So, I asked if he was Joe Jones. He said "no," and I said I had the wrong number.

Lieberman: And . . .

Franzen: I just waited, figuring maybe he'd come out for a walk or something.

Lieberman: And he did?

Franzen: After an hour maybe.

Lieberman: Can you describe the house?

Franzen: It was a house. That's all.

Lieberman: Go on.

Franzen: He walked down Sheridan Road to Morse and then toward the lake. I followed him. He just went to the beach and stood there looking at the water. It was getting dark. There were some people around, but they left.

Lieberman: Go on.

Franzen: I killed him.

Lieberman: How?

Franzen: Sidewalk near Morse is cracking. Chunks of concrete all over. I picked one up, a big one, came behind him, and hit him in the head.

Lieberman: He went down.

Franzen: Yeah, I hit him again, but I think I killed him with the first hit. It worked out fine. He started it by the lake. I finished it by the lake.

Lieberman: What did you do with the piece of concrete?

Franzen: Heaved it in the water. Then I heaved the body in the water.

Lieberman: You didn't get your chance to beat him then?

Franzen: Didn't have to. He was dead.

Lieberman: Then?

Franzen: I went home. I walked.

Lieberman: You want to write all this out for me and sign it?

Franzen: Yes.

Lieberman: You think of anything else, you just put it in. Anything I can get you?

Franzen: Get that garbage in the corner out of here or put me in a clean room.

Lieberman: I'll see what I can do. I'll go get you some paper.

Franzen: I'm not a good speller.

Lieberman: I'll get you a dictionary.

Franzen: It won't help.

Lieberman: Just write it like it sounds. I'll be right back with paper and a pen.

Franzen: Don't forget the garbage.

Lieberman went to the corner of the room, picked up the almost overflowing trash can, and went through the door into the squad room. He put the can down, took a few steps to the left, and went into the soundproof observation room.

The lights were off, but there was enough light from the interrogation room for the three detectives to see each other.

"He's either one hell of a smart con artist or he didn't kill Sokol," said Kearney.

"I don't think he's a con artist," said Hanrahan, looking at Franzen through the mirror.

Franzen was still seated, but he was looking back at the corner where Lieberman had picked up the garbage.

"I don't think so either," said Lieberman.

"Okay," said Kearney with a sigh. "His confession is full of shit. Wrong name for the victim, saying Sokol lived in a house. We could get around that, but that crap about a piece of concrete . . . Sokol's head was bashed in with something smooth and definitely wooden. Pieces were in his scalp. Whoever killed him also hit him in the face and kicked him or punched him hard on his chest and stomach. There was no piece of concrete in the water with blood on it. No bat or piece of wood either. So . . ."

"He didn't do it," said Lieberman.

"But he confessed to his friends," said Kearney, leaning

NOT QUITE KOSHER   199

back against the wall and folding his arms. "And to you."

"Wanted to take credit for it," said Hanrahan.

"Stand-up guy," said Kearney with a sigh.

"Martyr," said Lieberman.

"Friends turn him in, and he still wants them to think he did it," said Hanrahan. "What kid of a kid thinks like that for Christ's sake?"

"Nobody thinks like that for Christ's sake," said Kearney. "It's for his own sake. So, what do we have?"

"A very sloppy liar," said Lieberman.

"What does that leave us?" asked Kearney.

"The other two," said Lieberman.

"And El Perro," said Hanrahan.

Lieberman didn't answer. Something struck him, not hard but a small slap of memory.

"Hell of a coincidence," he finally said. "Sokol gets killed, and one of the hundreds of bad guys is someone we deal with."

"It happens," said Kearney.

"I think we need some search warrants," said Lieberman. "Judge Roscoe reachable?"

Kearney nodded yes. Albert Samuel Roscoe was one of the people who had stood by Kearney when the Shepard disaster had taken place. Albert Samuel Roscoe had great sympathy for the working police. Albert Samuel Roscoe gave out search warrants the way child molesters gave out candy. Albert Samuel Roscoe, who was dangerously close to retirement, was the policeman's friend, always willing to overlook the narrow niceties of the law.

"I'll give him a call," said Kearney. "Where you want to look?"

Lieberman told him. Kearney and Hanrahan exchanged glances.

"That's a stretch, Rabbi, even for Roscoe," Hanrahan said.

"You sure about this, Abe?" asked Kearney.

"No," said Lieberman.

When Kearney headed back to his office, Lieberman told a uniformed cop talking to another cop to bring a pad and pen into Jamie Franzen, then stay with him while he wrote his confession.

"When he's done, don't put him in the lockup. Just have him sit on the bench. I'll ask Rodriguez to keep an eye on him."

The cop nodded and went in search of pen and pad.

"I think you're wrong on this one, Rabbi," said Hanrahan, as they waited for Kearney to arrange for the search warrants.

"You mean you hope I'm wrong, Father Murph."

"Yeah."

Hanrahan shrugged.

Kearney opened his office door. He motioned for Lieberman and Hanrahan, who sidestepped a cop in a hurry carrying a handful of papers.

"I'll have the search warrants first thing in the morning. Right now, get over to Van Buren and Aberdeen," he said. "Someone plowed a Lexus into a store. Car's been stripped, but uniforms on the scene found some little gold animals on the floor under the mat."

"We're on the way," said Lieberman. "The warrants?"

"I'm working on them," Kearney said, glancing around his squad room. He looked as if he were going to say something, but changed his mind and went back into his office.

"Your turn to drive," said Lieberman.

No farther. That was it. It was raining now. Raining hard. Pouring. Bullets of water that stung when they hit your open skin.

Wychovski sat on the cracked concrete stoop of a boarded-up three-story redbrick factory. He huddled, knees up, clutching them, shivering, trying to keep them from knocking together.

The rain came after him. He pulled back against the boarded-up door. It didn't help much. He watched the cars go by slowly, splashing, spraying in the daylight-clouded darkness. Thunder, wind, waves in the water of the rivulets that had formed on both sides of the street and ran into the drains.

To his right about a block down was the Chicago River. He could see the bridge.

He was not simply soaked. He was a sponge; his weight felt as if it had doubled. His legs wouldn't listen to his commands or pleas. He had a cold, the flu, pneumonia.

No people were on the street now. They had all found

shelter somewhere, somehow. Rain jabbed at his legs. He tried to pull himself into a tighter ball.

Across the street a solitary old man, small, black with a white beard, walked slowly, his hands plunged into the pockets of his green Army surplus raincoat.

Crazy son of a bitch, walking wounded, Wychovski thought.

The man stopped as if he had been called by a voice Wychovski couldn't hear over the pounding, drumming of the rain on the sidewalk and street and the whooshing and spray of the passing cars.

The old man turned and began crossing the street. He was heading toward Wychovski. For a few seconds after he had crossed the street the old man stood in front of the figure huddled in the doorway. The old man seemed oblivious to the rain.

Wychovski mustered a look that he was sure said, Keep walking you crazy son of a bitch. I'm in no mood for company.

The old man either took the look as an invitation or ignored it. He sat next to Wychovski, his legs straight out onto the sidewalk, ran thumping against his already soaked pants.

"Troubles?" asked the old man.

Wychovski said nothing.

Troubles? Hell no. The cops were after him for killing a cop. A guy with a shotgun was after him to blow him away. He was cold, coming down with something, too wet, weak, and tired to move, and not knowing where to go. He was definitely beginning to lose his sense of humor.

"Like to be someplace else?" the old man said gently.

Someplace else? St. Louis, Kansas City, Moscow, Shanghai, the fucking North Pole, a hospital in Oslo, Wychovski thought, but he said nothing.

"Wouldn't do much good," said the old man, reaching into his pocket.

Wychovski released his grip on his legs, ready. His arms were deadweights, but he could handle this skinny old man if he came up with a knife or a gun. They were only inches apart, bodies almost touching.

The old man pulled out a Magic Marker, a red Magic Marker, and half turned toward the damp boards nailed against the door behind them. He also pulled out a pair of glasses and propped them on his nose.

The little alcove was covered with graffiti—boards, door, walls in marker, some of it color. "Lawndale Raiders Eat Shit," "Phanesha Simms Sucks. Call Her. 343-3494," "Burn A Pig," "K.J. and Emma Two Gether," "I Clean Up My Own Shit." Not very creative, though some of it had been written with some skill, especially a few gang names: Devil Rats, Lost Boys, Men With Guns.

The old man found a space and wrote carefully, slowly as the rain beat down and cars sprayed and splashed and thunder boomed. People hit their horns. In the daytime darkness, car lights skimmed the alcove. A light show. Wychovski was sure he had a temperature.

The old man leaned back to inspect what he had written and with slow dignity put the top back on his marker and returned it to his pocket.

Wychovski looked at what the old man had written: "Embrace Infinity."

"Sometimes I write, 'Accept Infinity,' " the old man explained, putting his glasses back in his pocket. "Depends on the weather, how I'm feeling, and who I'm writing for."

Maybe Wychovski could crawl to another doorway. He considered it, but the rain, anticipating his possible move, beat down even harder.

"When I was a boy," the old man said, looking at the traffic as it passed, "I was afraid of the infinite. I was supposed to be in awe, but I was just flat-out scared. I liked the sky, the stars, but one of my worst experiences when I was about ten was going to the Adler Planetarium on a school field trip. In that dark room, looking up at the ceiling, moving deep into space, hearing that voice, deep, you know, saying it went on forever. You understand?"

Wychovski didn't understand. He didn't want to understand. He considered singing a song inside his head to block out the man whose voice was raised so his alcove partner could hear him over the onslaught of nature.

"Grew up afraid to fall asleep in big rooms. Had this dream where the room kept getting bigger, I kept getting smaller. Youngest of seven children. Slept in a bed with three brothers. They all dreamed of someday living alone. I felt comfortable when I was in that small bed in that small room with a body on both sides."

The man let out a sigh. From the corner of his eye Wychovski could see that the man was shaking his head and smiling.

"Grew up," the old man said. "Read a lot. Went to school. Right through. University of Illinois. English literature. Taught at Marshall High School. You go to college?"

"No," said Wychovski.

"Well, one day I read this book. Picked it up at a used book store for a quarter. Ragged trade paperback with the cover coming off. Something about the title. *One.*

That was what it was called. Turned out to be about Hindu and Buddhist myths and such. One story hit me. Right away. Right through my eyes, deep into my head. I was brought up storefront Baptist. Never believed it. Didn't like dressing up. But that book. That story. Man, a king, was afraid of the same thing I was, that he was a piece of nothing on a piece of nothing, that both he and the piece he was on would be around for no time at all. You with me?"

"Where the hell would I go?" asked Wychovski.

"You look sick. Want me to help you get to a hospital?"

"No."

"Where was I? Oh, this king started to reincarnate. Always something smaller. First a dog. Then a cat. Then a rat. Then a cockroach. Then a flea. He never made it to virus, or maybe he did. But each time he got smaller, he felt more like he belonged, like not being the king or a mouse or anything wasn't all that important. Hell, wasn't important at all. Well, eventually he became a simple cell, though that's not what the book called it. He just became part of everything. The whole universe. He was content. Buddhists call it Nirvana."

"I know," said Wychovski.

"Well, I read that story, and I wasn't scared of the universe anymore. I could sleep outside. Strange thing is that after I read that story I slept better, no bad dream, never. Don't know the connection, but I know there's one. We're all scared of something. Dying mostly. Being nothing. Or, put it another way, not being something."

Enough. Wychovski wanted the old man to get the hell out of his corner of hell.

"I figure I know what you're scared of," said the old man.

"What's that?" asked Wychovski, his teeth chattering.

"A man in a leather coat carrying a suitcase in one hand and a shotgun under that coat."

Wychovski look at the old man, who tilted his head down and looked at him as if he were looking over the glasses he was no longer wearing.

"Heard it in the neighborhood," said the old man. "Big news of the day. White man crashes his big new car into a store three, four blocks that way, gets out. Black man gets out after him, shoots at him, and the white man goes running."

"And you figure the white man is me?"

"And the black man is the one who's coming down the street over there with the suitcase and the shotgun under his leather jacket."

Wychovski jerked his head around and looked into the downpour. Dickerson was about a block away, dim, coming through the darkness and thunder, moving steady, a slight limp.

"Here," said Wychovski, forcing himself to his feet and reaching into his pocket.

The old man got up and helped Wychovski to his feet. From deep in his pocket Wychovski pulled out a small golden lizard. He handed it to the old man.

"Salamander," said the old man, examining the golden lizard. "Good luck sign."

The rain was stopping, definitely stopping. The thunder was far away. It was still raining but not as hard. If he hadn't seen him before, Dickerson definitely saw him now.

He stopped for an instant, his head aimed directly at Wychovski.

"Want me to stay and die with you?" the old man said.

"You're fuckin' nuts."

"I'm old, dying of cancer, a bad heart, and who knows what else. Might not be a bad way to go, and you'd have someone next to you so you wouldn't be so scared."

Agony weighed him down, but there was something left. Not much, but something. Wychovski began to stagger toward the bridge.

The old man put the salamander in his green raincoat pocket and started back across the street.

There was no one Wychovski could ask for help. He knew cops. They had decided by now that he had killed one of them. They would probably shoot him just as surely as Dickerson would.

He slogged his way so slowly, so heavy, so tired. The rain had stopped now. The rivers in the gutters on both sides of the street ran swiftly. He stepped in sidewalk pools, socks heavy, water sloshing in his shoes.

He didn't look back. The bridge. If he could make it to the bridge, he could jump in. Dickerson would take a shot at him, but he would have a chance. He still clung to that, a chance. He tried to move faster.

The cop in the doorway held out his hand. Nestled in his palm were a small golden porcupine and another animal Lieberman couldn't identify.

"I think it's a mongoose," said Hanrahan.

Lieberman looked at the Lexus, or what was left of it.

"They got out," said the young uniformed cop with a

mustache that made him look a few weeks older than his twenty-four years. "Black guy shot and took off after the white guy. Lots of witnesses. About an hour ago. Woman who lives two blocks that way and one block over gave me this one."

He pulled another little golden animal from his pocket. Lieberman took the tiny bird.

"One more," said the young cop, a magician in blue, going back into his pocket, this time pulling out a golden rabbit. "Got it from a guy who has a little store right down the street."

"Honest citizens," said Hanrahan.

"Who knows how many our Hansel has given out?" asked Lieberman.

The rain had stopped. People were coming back on the street to watch the show. A passing car almost hit a woman carrying a baby, honked his horn, and kept on going.

"Pardon me," a voice came from Lieberman's side.

He turned to see a little black man in a green raincoat. The man had a white beard and steady brown eyes.

"Mine is a salamander."

He held his palm open, revealing the treasure to the police.

"I believe the man who gave it to me is about to be shot," the old man said. "That way. By the bridge."

The uniformed cop motioned at his partner, who was trying to keep the small crowd back. They ran for their patrol car. Lieberman and Hanrahan moved to their unmarked car. Both cars sped off in the direction the old man had pointed to, leaving him alone, hand out, palm up, salamander resting on it. The old man pocketed the golden animal and moved on.

Wychovski was almost at the bridge. A few more feet. He didn't want to look back. Dickerson couldn't be far behind. He expected the sting of the pellets into his back and head, penetrating his skull, lungs, liver, every organ. He couldn't go over the side yet. Below him was the embankment and pieces of concrete, wood, broken bottles. A few more feet.

Cars passed. Their lights were still on, though the sun had suddenly come through the clouds. Bright day.

His sense of horror was worse than in the rainy darkness.

He had one leg over the railing when he looked back and saw Dickerson about twenty feet away.

"There are witnesses all around," said Wychovski.

"Chance I'll have to take," said Dickerson.

"My prints aren't on that gun. Yours are. The gun that killed Walter." Dickerson shook his head and laughed.

Poe, Wychovski remembered. He remembered the lines he had memorized in his cell. Poe always sounded good. Sometimes he gave a chill.

" 'And as the Demon made an end of his story, he fell back within the cavity of the tomb and laughed,' " Wychovski said to himself. " 'And I could not laugh with the Demon, and he cursed me because I could not laugh.' "

Dickerson took a step closer.

"I took it from you when you crashed the car after taking me hostage. I came looking for you. You killed my boss. You're a cop killer. You've got a gun. I'll catch a little shit, but I'll be a hero."

"I don't have a gun," said Wychovski.

"You will after I blow your ass away," he said. "I've got one for you, your Glock."

"You'll lose everything," said Wychovski.

"Didn't have to be this way," Dickerson said. "But I'll take what I can get. I'll take over Walter's business and turn in what you stole. Wouldn't be surprised if I did get a medal. You got a name?"

"Wychovski, George Wychovski. You?"

"Dickerson, Robert."

Dickerson raised his shotgun. Cars zipped past. Wychovski could see eyes turn toward the scene, then turn away as the cars moved even faster. Wychovski heard them first and saw them first. The patrol car and the unmarked car heading toward them. The patrol car. Both cars were flashing their red lights. The patrol car turned on its siren.

Wychovski leaned over the railing. He knew he didn't have the strength to climb over. As he started to go over, Dickerson fired. A pepper of pellets drilled into the falling man's legs. Hot pain like the long deep scratches of a dozen cats.

He fell. But it didn't feel as if he were falling. He could see the sky. He had the sensation of rising. Embracing the infinite. Accepting the infinite. The sensation lasted about a second. He hit the dirty water hard. His breath escaped, and he began to sink. His clothes weighed him down, and he couldn't move his legs. They had no feeling. He flayed with his arms but kept going down.

The two cars stopped at the end of the bridge. The uniformed cops got out of their vehicle and leveled their weapons from behind their open doors. Lieberman and Hanrahan did the same.

"Put it down slowly," called Lieberman.

Dickerson put down the suitcase and the shotgun.

"Now, clasp your hands behind your head and look right at me."

Dickerson obeyed, and Hanrahan dashed toward the low fence at the end of the bridge. He scrambled over it and slid down the embankment, tearing his pants, scratching his palms. He almost slid into the rushing river but stopped at the wooden pilings.

Hanrahan caught his breath and looked toward the water. Wychovski had been carried more than thirty feet away. Hanrahan searched for some sign as he took off his jacket and holster and kicked off his shoes. He searched. Nothing.

Wychovski was still struggling. He frantically pulled watches out of his pocket, jettisoned whatever he had in his pockets, tried to hold his breath. He couldn't, however, fish out the last of the golden animals. He gave up trying for them. He gave up trying for anything, closed his eyes, and let the filthy water into his mouth.

Noah's ark was sinking. The end of the world had come. The animals went down not two by two but one by one. He embraced the infinite. What choice did he have?

When Lieberman got home just before seven, he took off his shoes, put them in the front closet, and looked over at his granddaughter. Before coming home he had stopped at the drugstore on Touhy and California to make a phone call. He didn't want to use his cell phone, and he didn't want to make the call from home. He had reached Emiliano "El Perro" Del Sol and explained what he wanted.

"*Por supuesto, Viejo.* Now you owe me another one."

"No," Lieberman had said. "I think you still owe me about five or six, but I'm not keeping count."

El Perro had laughed and said, "*Tan loco, mi amigo.*" Then he hung up, and Lieberman had gone home.

Melisa was sitting in the living room reading a book and watching television at the same time. Well, she wasn't actually sitting. She was sprawled on her back with one leg on the seat of his leather armchair and the other on the floor. She was watching something with a laugh track. From her position, she was watching it upside down.

"Grandpa," she said, scrambling to a sitting position. "They're coming."

"Who?"

"The Pink Cheek sisters," Melisa said, holding the book open on her lap.

"Pinchuk," Lieberman corrected, walking into the room.

"I know," Melisa said. "I'm being funny."

"They do have pink cheeks," Lieberman conceded, moving toward her with his arms open.

The girl placed the book facedown on the floor and moved into her grandfather's arms.

With Lisa, his daughter, it had never really been like this. Lisa had read. Lisa had seldom watched television. Lisa was not a hugger. Lisa had called him "Abe," not "Pop" or "Dad" or "Father" or "Abba."

His granddaughter's face was pressed against his chest, her arms tight around his waist.

"What are you reading?" he asked.

"One of your books," she said.

"Which one?" Abe asked, looking into the brightly lit dining room, which was set up for four people, which meant Rose and Esther were not joining them for dinner, just for dessert and harassment. No, that wasn't fair. They were there to help, and Lieberman was ultimately grateful for their assistance. He had simply had a long tough day, and, if he were right, tomorrow would be even harder.

They had taken Dickerson in, booked him on everything from murder, grand theft auto, grand theft, carrying a loaded shotgun, firing said shotgun on a city street, and leaving the scene of an accident, to obstructing traffic. There would be no chance of bail on this one.

Wychovski's body had been recovered more than a mile from where he had gone into the river. Kearney had called the widow of the dead jeweler and the widow of the dead cop. Alan Kearney had been taking on such calls for more than a year. Hanrahan and Lieberman agreed that he was doing some kind of psychological penance or maybe finding some solace in comforting people who had even sadder stories than he did. Though he wasn't responsible, Kearney carried the guilt of his own partner's death, a death that ended Kearney's promising future.

"I'm reading *War and Peace*," she said, stepping back to look up at him with a pleased grin.

"You understand it?"

"Not really," she said. "Too many people with Russian names. Too many big words. It's a challenge. It was the fattest book you had. I wanted to read the fattest. That one or the unabridged copy of Stephen King's *The Stand*."

"Unabridged," said Lieberman. "I suggest you put off the challenge of both books for a few years."

"Good. I'll read one of the Harry Potters again."

"Better," said Abe. "Where's your grandmother?"

"In your room."

"Barry?"

"In his room, working on his Torah portion," she said, moving into his chair. Her feet dangled. She bounced.

"You have no homework?"

"Did it. Easy," she said. "I told you, my school underestimates us."

"That's bad," he said.

"No, I like it that way."

"I see your point."

Lieberman walked through the living room to the bedroom door and stepped in. He closed the door behind him. Bess was wearing a blue robe and drying her hair with a bath towel.

"The sisters are coming," she said, as he removed his jacket, took off his holster and gun, and locked them in the drawer next to the bed with the key he wore around his neck.

Only then was she ready to meet him for a kiss. Bess was a good kisser. She felt after-shower warm and smelled like some flower he couldn't place.

"News of the day," she said. "Lisa and Howard will pay for the flowers at the bar mitzvah, the flowers on the *be-mah*, and the ones for the Oneg on Friday and the Kiddush on Saturday afternoon."

"Good news," said Lieberman.

"Todd and his wife are definitely not coming," she said, rubbing her hair, which was still quite naturally dark and shiny.

"Barry know?"

"Yes. He's relieved."

"More good news," Lieberman said, sitting on the bed and removing his wet socks.

"Something's on your mind," Bess said.

"The Pinchuks are coming."

"That's not it," she said, still drying her hair but keeping her eyes on him.

"We found the man who killed the policeman in Skokie," he said.

Dead policemen were not one of Bess's favorite subjects.

"He drowned in the Chicago River," he said. "It'll be on the news. We can watch at ten."

"There's something else, Abe. I've got dinner on. I've got to get us fed before Rose and Esther get here. Tell me, or you know I'll keep after you till you do."

"Something I have to do tomorrow, maybe," he said.

"Something I hope I'm wrong about. I'll tell you when I know."

"For now, I'll accept that if you don't brood," she said, moving toward the closet and dropping the towel onto the chair in the corner.

"Brooding is over."

"Dinner is in twenty minutes."

"And?"

"Baked chicken with sweet potatoes."

"Skinless?" he asked, wiggling his toes.

"Skinless," she called from the closet where she was pulling out a solid blue dress. "Thai peanut sauce. Low cholesterol sugar-free chocolate pudding for dessert. I plan to keep you alive, Avrum, in spite of yourself. Give me a hand."

"With the dress or my diet?" he asked.

"Both," she said.

A minute or so later Lieberman climbed the narrow stairway. He could hear his grandson's voice in his room. Barry's voice hadn't changed yet.

Lieberman could not understand Hebrew, but he knew Barry was working on his portions for the bar mitzvah. Barry would have to read a section of the Torah in Hebrew, the section for that Sabbath weekend. He would not only have to read it but to chant it with the proper traditional trope. The Torah is the first five books of the Holy Scriptures. Each year Jews read the Torah through at services from start to finish, and when they get to the end they have a celebration holiday, Simchas Torah, and immediately begin again.

In addition to chanting from the Torah, Barry would have a designated chanted reading from the Haftorah, that part of the Scriptures that comes after the Torah. Barry's reading was from Ecclesiastes.

"Come in," Barry called, when Lieberman knocked.

Lieberman found his grandson seated in front of his computer. On the screen was whatever he had been working on in Hebrew letters.

Melisa looked like her mother. Barry looked like his father, which meant he looked nothing like Lieberman. Barry was as tall as his grandfather and broader. He had escaped the Lieberman downcast face and not been blessed with Bess's beauty, but he was a good-looking boy who could have passed for a Swede or a Norwegian.

Lieberman smiled. It wasn't much of a smile, but it wasn't sardonic, resigned, or cynical. It reflected his sincere joy in his grandson.

"Dinner ready?" Barry asked.

"No," said Lieberman, moving to the wooden chair next to Barry. "We've got twenty minutes. Can you check some things for me on the Internet?"

"Police business?" Barry asked seriously.

"Some of it," Lieberman conceded. "Some of it temple business."

Barry pushed some buttons and moved the computer mouse.

"What do you need?"

"Can you get old newspaper articles on the Internet?"

"A lot."

"See what you can find on me," said Lieberman. "Then see if you can get me some office phone numbers for Joseph Lieberman. The one I've got is wrong."

"The senator?"

"Yes."

Barry had already been told that Joe Lieberman wasn't a relative, but he liked the idea that the senator and almost vice president had made the family name well-known and acceptable and even a little famous.

It didn't take Barry twenty minutes to find both of the things that his grandfather had asked for. He printed out a few of the documents, finishing just as Melisa came through the door after knocking but not waiting to be invited in.

"Dinner," she said.

She left the room, door open, and went down the stairs. Lieberman took the sheets of paper. He had hoped he had been wrong, but the sheets in his hand, while they did not prove him right, certainly made his theory a real possibility.

When Hanrahan got to his house, the dog was sitting on the porch, waiting.

Hanrahan grinned. He was an ugly mutt, a mongrel, big, white, and gray, shaggy. He was not Hanrahan's dog. He didn't even have a name. Lieberman and Hanrahan had saved him from the Humane Society. The dog was not young. He had been particularly wary of people, but Lieberman and his partner had treated him with dignity in the alley where a man had been murdered, and Hanrahan had reluctantly taken him home.

The dog now had a collar on which was written simply "Dog" and Hanrahan's address. The dog was free to roam outside or come in the house and be fed or sleep. Sometimes Hanrahan didn't see him for days. Sometimes he would come every day for a week or more.

"Well," Hanrahan said, opening the door. "You don't seem to have any new wounds or scars. I've got a few."

The dog listened intently as they went through the door.

"Tore my legs some and cut my hands," Hanrahan said, holding his hands out.

The dog sniffed at his palms.

"It's a long story," Hanrahan said, taking off his shoes and putting them on the mat near the door. "Maybe I'll tell you later if I don't start thinking I'm going a little nuts talking to a canine."

The furnishings in the small two-story house were old but clean. The house was immaculate. Bill Hanrahan kept it that way. At first he had done it in the hope that his wife, Maureen, would return someday and find that he had kept it as clean as she had and as ready for her return as he was. He had driven her away with his drinking. She hadn't had much choice other than risk the wrath of God or be a good Catholic wife and stand by him, watching her life pass and having no effect on her husband. While they had made peace with each other, Hanrahan was sure his former wife would never fully forgive him for making her go against the Church.

Hanrahan had joined AA, even returned to the Church himself, but it had been too late. Both of their grown sons had sided with their mother. They had witnessed the truth. Maureen had divorced him even though the Church had made it clear that there would be no annulment granted. Even then Hanrahan had hoped she would change her mind.

He had given up hoping three years ago and been drinking again when he met Iris at the Black Moon while he was watching an apartment building. He had been drunk on duty. Should have lost his badge, but Lieberman had covered for him and, for reasons he still didn't understand, the beautiful Chinese woman who waited on him sensed something in him that he didn't sense himself.

Now he was straight and sober, back in the Church, and about to be married. He would have said all this to the dog as he filled the big yellow bowl in the kitchen with Dog Chow, but the dog had already heard it more than once. The plan for the evening was simple. Call Iris. See if there were any last-minute changes or needs for the wedding, eat a cold leftover meat loaf sandwich with a Coke, take off his clothes, have a bath, clean his wounds, and go to bed early.

The doorbell rang when he opened the refrigerator.

Hanrahan had no children in his house, and there was no danger of the dog getting his paws on his guns and firing one of them. Hanrahan kept several weapons nearby. He had reasons. He had killed one intruder to the house a few years ago, a lunatic he had lured there for the express purpose of ridding the world of him and saving the madman's wife and small son from being his next victims. Twice, Laio Woo had come to the house to try to persuade him to give up his relationship with Iris. One of those times Woo had been in the house with two of his men in the kitchen when Hanrahan got home. One time Woo had come to the door with his men to warn him about his relationship with Iris. The next time Woo or a dozen of his men came to the door, he might not be coming to do any talking.

Hanrahan had his weapon in his right hand behind his back when he stood to the side of the door and asked, "Who is it?"

"Morales," the voice came. "El Perro sent me."

Hanrahan opened the door and backed away. In front of him stood a young man in a blue blazer, navy slacks,

white shirt, and red tie. He was tall, reasonably good-
looking, and holding his hands together in front of him
waist high.

Behind him Hanrahan could hear the dog growling
softly.

"Mother and father's anniversary," the young man explained, seeing Hanrahan examine his clothes. Then his
eyes turned to the dog. "Thirty-eight years."

"Congratulations," Hanrahan said. "To what do I owe
the pleasure."

"Can I come in?" the young man asked.

"It's a warm enough night," said Hanrahan. "We can
talk here. Besides, the dog doesn't like visitors."

"Okay. Let's keep the dog happy."

"You alone?"

"Car down the street," the young man said, looking over
his shoulder.

The young man had no accent at all. Hanrahan had
never met a Tentaculo who didn't have an accent either
brought with him from Puerto Rico, Mexico, Cuba, or
someplace else or acquired in the ghettos of Chicago where
Spanish was the first language. It wasn't unusual to come
across a young boy or girl who spoke no English even
though they had been born in the city.

"And what can I do for you, Morales?"

"For me? Nothing. It's what El Perro is doing for you."

Hanrahan waited.

"That Chinese guy this morning. El Perro did some
checking. He works for Woo the Chink. Woo the Chink
doesn't like you."

"I'm aware of that fact," said Hanrahan.

"You're marrying a chink woman," Morales said.

"A Chinese woman," Hanrahan corrected.

"Right. Sorry. Looks like Woo doesn't want you marrying her."

"So?"

"So, we're going to have some guys sort of watching out for you. They'll be cruising tonight or parked or strolling. They'll be there till you get married. El Perro figures after you're married, Woo will realize he's lost and back off."

"That's the way El Perro figures?"

Morales shrugged. The dog was growling louder now.

"He just wanted me to tell you so you don't spot our guys and shoot them or arrest them or something."

"El Perro doesn't like me," said Hanrahan.

"He doesn't like you a lot," said Morales with a smile. "But *El Viejo* is his friend. You're *El Viejo*'s partner."

"What if I tell you I don't want any protection?"

"I'm supposed to tell you you're getting it anyway and it won't cost you a dollar. You got a gun behind your back and a mean dog behind you, but they don't stop maybe three or four chinks with automatic weapons."

"And what does El Perro want in exchange?"

"Nothing," said Morales, looking at his watch. "They offended him by coming into his territory. Hey, look. I've got to go. You do what you want. I delivered my message."

"Anything else?" asked Hanrahan.

"Yeah, you look like shit. Dog go after you?"

"Long story," Hanrahan said, "and I already told it to the dog."

Morales sauntered down the steps, and Hanrahan closed the door.

He locked the door and moved back to the kitchen. The dog remained at the front door in a crouch, growling softly.

"He's gone," said Hanrahan. "How'd you like to try some meat loaf?"

The dog followed him into the kitchen. Hanrahan took out the plate, removed the layer of Saran Wrap, cut off a chunk of meat loaf for himself and one for the dog. He threw the dog's into the air. The dog's piece was devoured before it hit the floor.

Z and Eddie celebrated by having two Big Macs each and two bottles of beer in Eddie's trailer. Z's father had come to the police station with a briefcase full of papers he had placed on the desk of Alan Kearney. Neither Z nor Eddie had been present.

There wasn't enough to hold either of them, and Kearney knew that there would be a pretty good case for false arrest if he didn't let them go. It wasn't worth the effort. He knew where to find them.

"They're material witnesses," Kearney had said, knowing he would fall back but wanting some promise or commitment on the record and in his notes.

"They will both be available to a grand jury and for trial," Andrew Zembinsky had said. "And I understand that the young man who committed the murder has confessed, confirming what my clients have told you."

"He confessed," said Kearney, sitting back while the lawyer stood.

What Kearney failed to say was that the confession was useless. He could hold Franzen, but even a shiny new public defender could get him off on minimum or low bail.

Why not let these two walk thinking they were clear? They would have no reason to run, and Lieberman and Hanrahan could keep digging, harassing.

"I'll release them," Kearney said, patting the stack of papers Andrew Zembinsky had placed on his desk. "You have them ready to testify."

"I will," said Zembinsky, snapping his briefcase shut.

Kearney looked at the man standing on the other side of his desk. Zembinsky was a solid man in a dark suit that showed wrinkled signs of his having been through a long day. His dark hair could have used a comb, and his face was at four o'clock on the shave scale. He wore a tie but it was knotted loosely. The man looked bone tired.

"Can I tell you something?" Zembinsky said. "Off the record?"

"Yes as long as it's nothing that could incriminate any of them," Kearney answered, folding his hands on his desk, reminding himself of Father Gellen when Alan Kearney had come to him after Kearney's world had fallen apart.

"I don't like my son," the man said, shaking his head and smiling painfully. "Haven't liked him for the past four or five years. My wife and I haven't raised him badly. Or maybe we have. I don't think so. He wasn't particularly spoiled or punished. Somehow he gradually became the kind of kid parents want their kids to stay away from. You have any kids?"

"No," said Kearney.

"I'll give him one thing," Zembinsky said. "Through all the crap he has been into, he's never asked for my help. I wouldn't be here now if it wasn't for my wife. I don't think she has any more love for Melvin than I do, but she feels a lot more guilt. She's not sure why. My son is going to walk out of here, not come home, not call his mother, and not thank me."

"Some kids are just born that way," said Kearney. "Nothing much you can do to stop it. My sister was like that. But my father spoiled her. He was a cop."

Kearney didn't know what his father having been a cop had to do with his sister's history of defiance, but Kearney somehow felt the connection.

Zembinsky reached out his hand and Kearney stood to shake it. The lawyer's grip was firm but not trying to prove anything.

"Thanks for listening," said Zembinsky.

"My job," answered Kearney.

And the lawyer left quickly.

Z and Eddie were unaware of the conversation. All Z knew was that his father had gotten him out without being asked. He owed neither of his parents thanks.

"No one asked to be born," he said, holding his beer bottle up for a toast.

Eddie clinked his bottle up to meet Z's.

"Nobody asked," he said.

There was a knock at the door.

"Gina," Eddie guessed. "You feel like Gina tonight?"

"No," said Z. "If she brought her black friend, what's her name?"

"Matty," said Eddie, moving toward the door, bottle in one hand, leering back at Z.

"Then it's different," said Z. "If not, tell her you just got tested for HIV and you're waiting for the results."

"I'll tell her you got tested, and you're the one waiting for the results."

Z's head hurt like a son of a bitch. Even if Matty did

come through the door, he doubted that he could do anything about it. The beer wasn't helping. Pain suddenly shot through the side of his head away from the stitched wound.

As Eddie opened the door, Z felt like saying he thought he should go back to the hospital.

The door blocked Z's view. Eddie said nothing. There was no greeting from Gina or whoever was there.

"Who is it?" Z called, putting down the beer bottle, feeling definitely sick to his stomach.

The door pushed open all the way, revealing Jamie Franzen. Jamie stood with his feet apart, a baseball bat in his right hand.

"Join the party," Eddie said carefully. "We're celebrating. They let us all out. We're clear."

Z didn't like this, didn't like the dull, distant look on Jamie's face. What the hell was Jamie doing out? He had confessed. Eddie and Z were going to testify. And what the hell was he doing with that bat?

"They didn't believe me," Jamie said, still standing in the door.

"Didn't believe what?" asked Eddie nervously.

"Didn't believe I killed Sokol. You both turned me in, but they didn't believe me. I told them I did it. They didn't believe me. I stood up for you."

"We knew they'd let you out," said Z, closing his eyes. He thought he tasted blood in his mouth. "We were celebrating, waiting for you. Have a beer."

Eddie backed away, eyes on the bat.

"Wanna know what I see?" asked Jamie. "I see two beers and two empty Big Mac boxes. You didn't know they were letting me out."

"We thought they were letting you out in the morning," Eddie tried.

"You killed that Sokol," Jamie said. "You killed him, and when I told you I did it to show off to you, make you think I had balls, you turned me in."

"We didn't kill him," Z said, sitting back on the couch. "We thought you did. We believed you."

"And you turned me in. I don't believe your lying mouth," Jamie said calmly. "I don't want you anymore."

"Sorry you feel that way," Eddie said, looking to Z for help. Z was the talker. He needed Z's mouth, but Z looked like shit. His eyes were dancing.

Jamie stepped in and swung the bat at Eddie. The blow cracked Eddie's arm. Z could hear it, could hear Eddie scream in pain as Jamie moved across the room. Z could see Eddie running out the door.

He tried to get up.

"Stop a second," Z tried, shaking his head. "We can talk. I can explain."

Jamie brought the bat down with all his might on Z's head as the seated young man tried to stand up. The bat against Z's skull made the sound of a hammer hitting a coconut. That's what Z thought. That was the last thing he thought. The coconut. The hammer. He must have been seven or eight. His father and he had drained the coconut of cloudy milk and they had taken turns smashing at it as it skittered across the concrete floor of the garage. They had chased it like a trapped animal, taking turns, laughing, having a good time.

If he lived, he'd describe it that way to his father.

But he didn't live.

The Hollywood Linen Shop was in the Old Orchard Shopping Center in Skokie off of Skokie Boulevard. It was a sprawling mall of midscale and upscale stores and a few restaurants. It had been one of the first malls in the area and had undergone frequent changes. Shops came and went. New ideas were tried. One place tried to specialize in chocolate-covered pretzels and twenty flavors of popcorn. It lasted almost a year.

But the Hollywood Linen Shop had been in the same location on the south end of the mall for almost thirty years.

Lieberman had the warrant in his pocket. He preferred not to use it and probably wouldn't have to, but it didn't hurt to have it.

Lieberman and Hanrahan had met at the T&L just before eight in the morning before going into the Clark Street Station to pick up the warrants.

"Abe tells me it's the big day," Maish had said, serving them coffee at their regular booth.

"The big day," Hanrahan had agreed.

"I'll have the food at Abe's house all set up after the wedding. Your favorites."

"Won't be many people," said Hanrahan. "We're keeping it small."

"Make it bigger," said Maish, hovering over the table. "Terrell's got a special today. Fried kosher salami and grilled onion on a toasted bagel."

"I'll take it," said Hanrahan.

"Should I even bother to second the motion," asked Abe, "or am I going to be consigned a bowl of oatmeal?"

"Exception today," said Maish. "Special occasion. In honor of your partner's wedding. But no butter. If I catch you putting butter or jelly on the sandwich, I break your arm."

"I can live with a broken arm," said Lieberman.

"Can you take my order, Maish?" a voice called behind them.

The T&L breakfast crowd was rolling in. Maish waited the tables himself and handled the cash register. He was dumpy, overweight, and, like his brother, looked a decade older than he was, but when he moved inside the T&L he had the full-court-press speed and efficiency he had displayed for three undefeated seasons back at Marshall High.

Maish turned to the Alter Cocker table, where Al Bloombach, Sy Weintraub, and Howie Chen sat waiting. It had been Bloombach who had called out to Maish.

"The usual?" asked Maish over the talking of the nine other customers on the counter stools, in the booths, and at the tables.

"I'm living dangerously," called Bloombach. "I'll have the special. Extra salami."

Howie and Sy said nothing. Sy was still in his sweatsuit.

He was somewhere in his eighties, but he ran every day, rain or shine. In the winter he ran laps around the gym at the Bernard Horwich Jewish Community Center. He didn't jog. He ran, not fast, but there was no doubt it was running. His "usual" was decaf coffee, two eggs scrambled, orange juice, and a toasted bialy. He would have no part of bagels. He was a loyal bialy man. Howie's usual was a lox omelette.

"See the paper?" Bloombach said, holding the *Sun-Times* up and open to an inner page. "You're famous again."

Lieberman had seen the paper at home. He had been up at five to take it from the front steps and retire with it to the kitchen, where he heated coffee and had time to read before he woke Bess and the kids.

It had been a good night for Lieberman. Four hours sleep, maybe a little more. He had soaked in the tub till his thin body gave up and wrinkled. He had added hot water four or five times while he read a book about Bruno Bettelheim. He didn't even bother to go to bed till a little after midnight. When he awoke a few minutes before five, he got up as quietly as he could. Sometimes he simply lay there next to Bess, waiting for first light. He had no illusions about getting back to sleep.

He had dreamt, but he didn't remember his dream or dreams, only that they had been there. All in all it had been a better than average night.

The article was small, five paragraphs buried on page eight. It told about the incident on the bridge, the bizarre death of the cop killer, and it speculated on the connection to the death of the jeweler and the antique dealer. Lieberman's name and Hanrahan's were in the article.

"Fame is fleeting," said Sy Weintraub.

Howie and Al looked at the old man. Sy Weintraub seldom spoke at the Cockers' table and when he did people listened.

"Fame is fleeting?" said Bloombach. "I'll write that one down so I don't forget to tell Rosen when he gets here. You get that from one of Howie's fortune cookies?"

"Everything is fleeting," Weintraub said seriously, ignoring Bloombach's attempt at wit.

"I'll drink to that," said Howie.

The three Alter Cockers raised their coffee mugs. So did Lieberman, Hanrahan, and some of the patrons who had heard the words of wisdom.

"*La Chaim*," said Sarah Bass, who more than filled the stool on which she sat at the counter. Sarah was seventy-three, an honorary Alter Cocker who was allowed minimal participation in the group of old men, who had an unalterable and unofficial rule that only men could sit at the table and that during the morning hours wives were not permitted in the T&L. This was fine with the wives. There had been one exception. Sol Mandelbaum's wife Rose had come one morning five years earlier and sat at the counter drinking tea and tearing with her teeth at an egg bagel with cream cheese.

Rose was angry with Sol. No one knew why. Neither Sol nor Rose talked about it. She simply sat there, ate, drank, and glared. There had been no conversation at the Alter Cocker table that morning. Sol Mandelbaum had left after a quick cup of coffee. He left his bagel with cream cheese untouched.

Rose never returned to the counter but Sol, a retired insurance salesman, had suffered the slings and arrows of the table for more than two years, acquiring the nickname "the Henpeck Man."

Abe and Bill ate in silence. Bustling from customer to customer, Maish kept an eye on his brother to be sure he wasn't shmeering cream cheese or grape jelly.

"The Tentaculos can't watch me forever, Rabbi," Hanrahan had said.

"Woo is a realist," said Lieberman.

"Woo is one angry, tough old bastard is what he is," said Hanrahan.

"You're not changing your mind again?" asked Lieberman, savoring his treat with small bites that he chewed slowly.

"Nope. It's on. I'm just saying . . ."

Hanrahan had hesitated.

"Maybe I should take early retirement and Iris and I should pack up and move away."

"It's an option," said Lieberman. "But that's not what you have in mind."

"After the wedding, I'm going to talk to Woo again," said Hanrahan.

"About what?"

"Survival and revenge," said Hanrahan. "He understands them."

"He specializes in them," said Lieberman. "But it's worth a try."

"No more Tentaculos," said Hanrahan. "We're not going to live under siege."

"I'll tell El Perro," said Lieberman. "Anything else for the wedding planner?"

"No."

"Then let's go."

Ten minutes later they had picked up their warrants from Kearney, who, again, looked as if he had spent the night in his office. His face was shaved. He wore a clean shirt, but he still had on the same slacks and jacket as the day before.

"Melvin Zembinsky is dead," Kearney had greeted them soberly. "Franzen beat his head in and broke Denenberg's arm. A reporter from WBBM picked it up, did some checking, talked to Denenberg, called me asking why a confessed murderer had been let loose to kill again. I told him I'd check with the chief and get back to him. Had five calls since from the newspapers and television. You don't talk to reporters on this one."

Lieberman and Hanrahan agreed.

"Franzen is in holding," Kearney said, going to his desk and picking up a coffee mug. He looked at the liquid, changed his mind, and put the cup back down. "He wants to talk, to confess. We've got a legal in there with him."

Kearney didn't have to say that the situation looked bad. These were white kids from good families. Zembinsky's father might sue the city, but Kearney had the feeling that he wouldn't. If they had been black kids, there wouldn't have been a story here. The papers would have made a little check mark next to the police report and assumed a dumb-ass fight over drugs, an affront, too much to drink. But white kids from decent families in a story like this were news.

Alan Kearney was once again going to take some heat. He had spoken to Terry Banovich downtown and the chief's assistant had cautiously suggested that the now-dead Melvin Zembinsky, with or without Denenberg, had killed

Sokol and tried to frame Franzen, who in a state of rage had effectively closed the case.

Kearney could probably get Denenberg to agree to dump the murder on his dead friend. The public defender could possibly be maneuvered to help Jamie Franzen remember Z's confessing the murder in exchange for a manslaughter plea. The state attorney might offer Franzen a deal he couldn't refuse in exchange for a lie. Or maybe it was true. Kearney didn't know. Lieberman was given the two warrants. They might turn up an even more sensational answer, might save Kearney's ass to fry another day.

And so Abe Lieberman and Bill Hanrahan, on a slightly overcast and cool May morning, entered the Hollywood Linen Shop and introduced themselves, showing their badges to a well-groomed woman in her thirties with short blonde hair, a clean, clear face, and thin lips she kept together to keep them from trembling.

"We'd like to see Mr. Sokol's books," said Lieberman.

"Why?" the woman asked.

"Well Miss . . ." Lieberman began.

"Mrs., Mrs. Althea Glick."

"It's routine," said Hanrahan.

Althea Glick looked confused. There were no customers in the store, which had opened only minutes before.

"I thought about closing today," she said, looking around at the tables and shelves of merchandise. "But . . . I wasn't sure what would be right."

"Opening is right," Lieberman said.

The shop smelled good, faintly flowery, completely clean.

"Life goes on," Althea Glick said. "Is that it?"

"Something like that," said Lieberman. "How's business been?"

"Business? The shop? We had a slight downturn last quarter, but we're back up. The other two Hollywood shops are about the same. I don't . . ."

"The company is losing money," Hanrahan said.

"The company is not losing money," Althea Glick said with a flash of pride. "We had a very good last year and overall a good one this year. Hollywood Linen is very healthy financially. Arnold, Mr. Sokol, has been talking about opening another store in Wheeling."

Lieberman and Hanrahan glanced at each other.

"The books . . ." Lieberman began.

". . . will confirm what I've just told you. Please follow me. There really are no books. Everything is on the computer, but I'll access whatever you need."

Althea Glick was going to protect her dead boss's reputation. No warrant was needed.

Twenty minutes later the detectives left the shop with thirty printed sheets inside a manila folder. There were seven customers, all women, in the shop when they left.

The baby, about three months old, was on his back in one of those bouncing seats. He was reaching for a dangling plastic ball in front of him. Once in a while he managed to make contact. The rattle of the ball seemed to startle him.

Lieberman and Hanrahan sat drinking their third cups of coffee of the morning. They sat across from Mary Sokol.

"Matthew is in school," she said, reaching over to touch the corner of the baby's mouth with a clean tissue.

They had needed no warrant here either. Mary Sokol had allowed them to look in the desk drawer in the bedroom.

Hanrahan had found some documents written by Sokol and brought them out to the living room.

He handed it to Lieberman along with some other papers. There was a computer on the desk with a speaker on each side. Cards with writing on them were stacked on the desk.

"I use the desk more than Arnold," she said. "My work. Arnold worked at the shop."

"Yes, ma'am," said Hanrahan. "We know."

"Would you like some coffee? I should stay with the baby."

"Coffee would be fine. These were written by your husband?"

He showed her the items, and she looked puzzled.

"Yes," she said. "Why?"

"Let's talk over coffee," Lieberman said.

The two policemen sat in the living room while the widow, dressed in a black dress, got the coffee. Hanrahan smiled at the baby, who took a beat to decide, then smiled back.

"Got a way with babies," he said.

"I scare them," said Lieberman.

"Well," said Mary Sokol, sitting back in the chair next to the baby, "I got a call early this morning. If I have it right, one of the men who beat him the other night stalked Arnold and killed him. And then you let him go, and he killed one of the other men who had beaten Arnold."

"It's not really clear yet," said Hanrahan.

"No," she said, looking at the baby. "Nothing is clear."

"Can we ask you some questions?" Lieberman said.

"Questions? Yes."

"One important one," said Lieberman. "I want you to

think about it, then I want to say something to you before you answer it."

"Yes," she said, brushing back her hair.

"Why did you kill your husband?"

Hanrahan was watching her closely. They both were. The widow seemed to have no reaction. She touched the cloth to the gurgling baby's mouth again and sat back.

Lieberman read her her rights and asked her if she understood. She said she did.

"You want a lawyer before you answer the question?" asked Hanrahan.

"No," she said.

Lieberman handed her the file from the Hollywood Linen Shop.

"Your husband's business isn't in trouble," he said. "It's doing very well. He didn't have to borrow money from anyone."

"I don't understand," she said.

"I've checked his appointment book," said Lieberman. "The one in his desk. The book is filled with entries. I've got these copies of your husband's handwriting. The entries in the appointment book were not written by your husband. They are close, but not close enough. We'll show them to an expert, but it doesn't take an expert to tell. I'm going to guess that you filled this appointment book."

Mary Sokol looked at Hanrahan.

"You sure you don't want a lawyer?" he asked.

"No lawyer," she said with a shake of her head, looking toward the window.

"You do research on the computer for a living," said Lieberman. "After you met me and my partner at the hospital, you had our names. You checked and found stories linking me with El Perro. My grandson did the same thing last night. You filled in that appointment book and gave it to my partner so we would go after El Perro."

"I went to confession this morning, early," she said, her face blank. "I took the baby after I took Matthew to school. One of the cleaning ladies who works at the church watched the baby. I confessed. The priest told me I should tell you what I did, but he absolved me. I couldn't just come and confess. I have two babies."

"How did you kill him?" asked Hanrahan.

"The children were asleep," she said. "Arnold was so depressed. He said he had to take a walk. I went with him. We weren't going to leave the children alone for more than ten or fifteen minutes. We talked about his medication, that he wasn't taking it. We walked down to the lake. I listened to him. I always listened to him. We were sitting on a bench just looking at the stars and the water and he told me he had to go away, had to start again. He said he was sorry. He cried. I consoled him. I was frightened. And then, suddenly, I was angry. He was going to walk away from me and our children. I got up and found the block of wood."

"And you hit him," Hanrahan said.

The baby hit the dangling plastic ball with a random swipe, and it rattled gently. Mary Sokol smiled at the infant.

"I hit him," she said, turning back to the policemen. "I hit him. I hit him again and he fell to the ground and I kept hitting him and hitting him."

"You hit him till he was dead," said Lieberman.

"I hit him till he was dead. Then I dragged him across the beach and pushed him into the water."

"You had it all planned?" Hanrahan asked.

"No," she said. "It just happened. He was crying, saying he was going to leave me and the children. I told him that it was a sin in the eyes of our Savior. He said he didn't believe in Jesus."

"And that's why you killed him?"

"I don't know. I don't think so. My sin in killing him was greater. I didn't plan to do it. I didn't do any planning till I got home and saw the children sleeping. Then I checked your name on the Internet and filled in the appointment book."

"Would you like more coffee?" she asked.

"No," said Lieberman.

"They're going to ask me more about why I did it, aren't they?" she asked.

"Yes," said Hanrahan.

"I don't have the answers," she said. "Don't you have people who do things, terrible things, and don't know why? Sometimes regular people like me?"

"Yes," said Lieberman.

"And they say we're crazy," she said with a sigh. "I'm a Catholic, but I don't believe in possession by demons or traps of the devil. And I'm not crazy. Maybe I was for a few seconds or minutes or hours, but I'm not crazy. Confession didn't help. A priest can't absolve me. I killed my husband. My children are going to be taken from me. If God forgives me, he can forgive anyone, and there are people, people even worse than I am, who should never be forgiven."

"You have someone who can watch the baby, pick up your son after school?" asked Lieberman.

She rose, moved to a corkboard in the kitchen, and removed a sheet of paper held by a pushpin. She brought the sheet into the living room and handed it to Hanrahan.

"It's a list of everything you'll need," she said, standing over them. "My sister's name, address, and phone number. A backup friend if you can't reach her. I've written a note for my sister. I'll get that. You can give it to her. There's nothing in it about what I did, just how to take care of the children and what to do with the apartment."

"You had this ready?" Hanrahan said heavily.

"I prepared it months ago," she said. "I expected her to use it when I died. I've been expecting death for a long time. I didn't expect this, didn't think about Arnold when I wrote it. As God is my judge. God punished me. He . . . I . . . I think I should call my lawyer now. His name is Charles Angotti. His number is on that sheet. I called him yesterday and told him I might be needing him sometime soon or in a little while."

There was something more than chilling in the woman's careful preparation, her resignation.

"You see," she went on, "I wouldn't have been able to let an innocent person go to prison for killing Arnold. I know that now. I knew it yesterday."

"Call your sister and your lawyer," Lieberman said. "We'll wait."

Mary Sokol nodded and moved to the telephone on the table against the wall. She picked up the phone and began punching the buttons. And then she stopped. She stood there with the phone in her hand and turned to the policemen.

"Could you? Please?"

She held the humming phone out to them. Hanrahan moved quickly to take it from her and lead her back to the chair next to the baby.

15

Lieberman did not believe in miracles. He did believe in coincidences. He had seen too many to deny their existence. Once he had gone out at two in the morning unable to sleep, unable to read, nothing on television to watch. He had gone out intending to go to Dunkin' Donuts, have a decaffeinated coffee and a plain donut, and talk to the night man or read an article or two in the *Smithsonian Magazine* he had rolled up in his coat pocket.

He didn't know what changed his mind, but instead of going to Dunkin' Donuts he stopped at a Denny's. When he walked through the door he saw that there was only one other customer in the place, William James Sinett.

Now that was where the coincidence came in. Lieberman had spent the day looking for William James Sinett in connection with a series of armed robberies. Sinett did not live in this neighborhood or anywhere near Rogers Park, nor had he committed any crimes that Lieberman knew of in the area. But there he was, sitting, having a cup of coffee, eating a large piece of some kind of cream pie.

After he had arrested Sinett, Lieberman had asked him why he had gone to this Denny's.

"I don't know," Sinett had answered. "I was just driving, and I felt like having a piece of pie."

Coincidence. But such things happened more than once in a person's lifetime.

After booking Mary Sokol, Kearney heard their story and wasn't sure whether to be happy that he was off the hook for letting Franzen and the others go the day before or he was sad because of what Mary Sokol had done.

"And that's her best reason?" he had asked, standing at the window of his office.

"That's all she gave us," said Lieberman.

"It's better than no reason," said Kearney. He had seen dozens, maybe a few hundred or more cases in which someone who seemed completely sane attacked or murdered someone else and could give no good reason for the crime. Kearney believed there was always a reason, but sometimes the criminal had no conscious idea of what it was.

That was the job of the shrinks. They would work on Mary Sokol. The prosecutor's psychiatrist. The defendant's psychiatrist. They'd both find reasons. Maybe the right one. Probably not.

"You're still getting married tonight?" Kearney asked.

"Tonight," said Hanrahan.

"I'll be there," said Kearney.

Hanrahan had expected Kearney to give an excuse.

"What are you two working?"

"Definite multiple arson," said Lieberman. "Last night. Two homeless people were killed. Hit-and-run on Lunt near Western. Victim's an old woman. She's in Ravenswood Hospital. Critical but alive."

Kearney nodded.

"Take the afternoon off," he said. "Both of you."

They thanked him and went into the squad room, which was a little less busy than the day before. The smell was no better, but the bodies were fewer.

"A superstitious man might say what we saw today was a bad omen," said Hanrahan, as they walked toward the door.

"What we saw today?"

"Mary Sokol. I'm getting married today, and I meet a woman who seemed to have a decent marriage, a Catholic woman, and she murders her husband. That strikes me like it might be an omen."

"You look for omens, you find them," said Lieberman. "Good and bad."

"So our coming down on Mary Sokol is just a coincidence?" Hanrahan asked, as they moved down the narrow stairs and into the lobby, where Nestor Briggs behind the desk nodded at them as he talked to two old men with beards who might have been twins.

"You made the connection, Father Murph. You remember me finding William Sinett? That was a coincidence. This is not, not a coincidence, not an omen. Maybe it's an excuse, but if it is, and I say this as your best man before I go home and put on my best suit, then don't use it. Don't blame it on God, magic, or chance. Do what you have to do and take responsibility. You want to get married?"

"I do."

"Then get married."

They moved into the parking lot. The sky was overcast, but it definitely didn't look or feel like rain. Lieberman and Hanrahan had both driven in to the station.

"Six o'clock," said Lieberman. "Unitarian church."

"I'll be there," said Hanrahan, pulling out a smile.

"Don't bring the dog."

"I won't bring the dog," Hanrahan said, moving to his car.

"Bring the ring," Lieberman said, calling across from his car.

"I'll bring the ring."

"Wear pants."

"I'll think about it," said Hanrahan.

"Good," said Lieberman.

Hanrahan drove away first. Lieberman, windows open, took out his notebook and removed his cell phone from his pocket. This was as good a time and place to do it as any. He dialed the number his grandson had found on the Internet.

"Senator Lieberman's office," came a woman's voice.

"My name is Abraham Lieberman. I'm a detective in the Chicago Police Department. How do I get to talk to the senator?"

"One moment please," she said.

Two minutes later a man's voice said, "Who are you and what is it you wish to speak to Senator Lieberman about?"

Lieberman repeated what he had said to the woman and added that he wanted to talk to the senator about a possible speaking engagement.

"Are you related to the senator?"

"I doubt it."

Lieberman explained to the man that the temple wanted him as a featured speaker at a luncheon, a dinner, a breakfast, anything and almost anytime the next month or the month after.

"Do you have a number where we can verify your identity?"

Lieberman gave him the station number.

"Ask for Lieutenant Kearney," he said.

"And is that the number where we can reach you?"

Lieberman gave the man his home phone number and cell phone number.

"And you said you're a Democrat?" the man asked.

"As a matter of fact," Lieberman said with a deep sigh, "I'm a registered Libertarian. If you want to know if I voted for Senator Lieberman, the answer is no. I voted for Harry Browne."

"Someone will get back to you, Detective," the man said abruptly.

"Thank you."

The man hung up. Lieberman had done his duty. He started to head home but checked his watch. There was a day game at Wrigley. He had forty-five minutes to make it. He could watch at least five innings before he had to go home and change. He turned out of the parking lot and headed south.

Hanrahan pulled over on his way home and called the Black Moon. There was no answer. He called Iris's home number. She answered.

"Haven't changed your mind?" he asked.

"No. Have you?"

"No. You sure you want to take a cab with your father?"

"I'll go with him and leave with you," she said.

"Sounds good to me. How's your father doing?"

"Resigned," she said. "He's afraid I'll try to have a baby. He thinks I'm too old. He thinks the baby might come out not looking the least bit Chinese. He wants his grandchild, should there be one, to be Chinese."

"We're not even married yet," he said. "And you're talking babies again."

"And that upsets you?"

"It used to," he said. "I'm not sure anymore. Can we put that one off for a little while?"

"Not long," she said. "If we decide to adopt a baby, it must be soon. My father is right. I'm too old."

"You are young and beautiful," he said. "You are perfect."

"I don't want to be perfect," she said. "It's too much work."

He laughed.

"See you at five at the church."

That was it. No turning back now. He didn't want to turn back. He didn't want a drink. He didn't want to think about Mary Sokol and her children. He wanted a long, very hot shower.

There were twelve people at the wedding, including the bride and groom. They gathered in the chapel, which was capable of comfortably holding 150 people though there had never been a service there approaching that number.

The minister was no more than forty, clean-shaven, a former Catholic priest. He had straight dark hair that dangled in a lock over his forehead. The minister's wife, who was also a minister, was there to greet people. She looked enough like the minister to be his sister.

Gathered were Abe, Bess, Maish, Yetta, Kearney, Iris's father and sister.

The minister's voice echoed in the emptiness of the hall. The lights had been left bright at Iris's request. She was dressed in white, not a wedding dress, but something that they all knew she had made with her sister's help. Hanrahan wore his best suit. His cheeks were pink from shaving closely. Lieberman thought his partner's knees looked a little uncertain, but Hanrahan had two bad knees that often failed to cooperate.

The service had been short, with a very brief few words of congratulations from the minister. Everyone shook hands, and the small motorcade headed back to the Lieberman house, where Terrell had laid out the food on the dining room table with the help of Barry and Melisa.

That was the part Hanrahan had expected.

What he didn't expect was that the small house would be full. Five of the Alter Cockers were there. Nestor Briggs was there. But most important, Hanrahan found himself facing his son Michael and not only his son but his daughter-in-law and his two grandchildren.

"Congratulations," Michael said, giving his father a hug, then doing the same to Iris.

"Congratulations, Bill," his daughter-in-law said, giving him a sincere smile and a hug and moving to Iris.

Hanrahan knelt to hug his two grandsons, who had been prepared for such an event, had been told about the grandfather who had not seen them since they were babies.

"Food's hot," said Herschel Rosen.

They were serving themselves from the buffet, talking in small and somewhat odd groups: Kearney and Sy Weintraub, Iris's father and Terrell, Maish and Yetta and Hanrahan's daughter-in-law. Howie Chen was lost in a serious conversation with the five-and six-year-old Hanrahan boys, and Barry and Melisa were talking to Iris.

Then the doorbell rang.

"Party crashers," said Bess, moving to the door.

When she opened it, there stood a young Chinese man, Ye, the young man who had confronted Lieberman and Hanrahan in the street in front of El Perro's bingo parlor.

The young man seemed to be dressed exactly and as neatly as he had the day before except today he wore no sunglasses.

Everyone went silent. Hanrahan stepped in front of Iris and Lieberman moved to his side. Neither of the policemen were armed.

The young man looked around the room from face to face, then stepped into the house and out of the way as a huge Chinese man entered hugging a massive, shiny black vase that must have been five feet tall. The vase was decorated with golden dragons and flowers.

"A wedding gift from Mr. Woo," the young man said. "He regrets that he is unable to deliver it himself."

The young man stepped forward and handed an envelope to Hanrahan, then backed away. He looked at Lieberman, who said, "You want a slice of brisket for the road?"

"I think not."

"Want us to make up a plate for Mr. Woo?" Lieberman asked amiably.

"Abe," Bess whispered at his side.

"Thank you, no," said the man, nodding to the huge man, who went back through the door. The young Chinese man nodded and left the house, closing the door behind him.

Hanrahan opened the envelope and read. He handed it to Iris and turned to Lieberman.

"It's over, Rabbi. He wishes us a long and happy life and marriage."

"You trust him?"

"He wouldn't do this if it weren't true," said Iris. "Mr. Woo is a criminal, but his word is better than a written contract."

People were gathering around the huge vase. Iris's father moved toward it, touched, and turned to his two daughters, saying something in Chinese.

"My father says this is a very valuable gift," Iris said.

"So far so good," said Hanrahan.

There was another knock at the door.

Abe opened the door. Emiliano "El Perro" Del Sol stood there, white box in hand. He was dressed in a suit.

"You cool with the chinks?" he asked Lieberman. "We were watching them to see if they started trouble."

"We are cool with Mr. Woo and his friends," said Lieberman.

El Perro looked around and saw Kearney.

"I can't stay," said El Perro. "Got places to go. Here Irish," he added, handing Hanrahan the box. "*Su esposa es tan bonita.*"

"He says Iris is beautiful," Lieberman translated.

"Thanks," said Hanrahan. "I can't take this."

"You took that big ugly piece of glass from the chink," El Perro said. "You can take this from me. Open it. Take a look."

Hanrahan opened the box and started to laugh.

"You don't want it, give it to someone. See you around sometime, *Viejo. Usted, tambien Irish.*"

And El Perro was gone.

"What is it?" asked Bess.

Hanrahan pulled a football from the box and turned it over.

"It's got Dick Butkus's and Mike Ditka's signatures on it," he said.

Hanrahan looked at Kearney, who shrugged.

"Keep it," said Kearney. "And the vase. I don't see a football and a big vase turning you into a rogue cop."

Everyone applauded.

This time the phone rang. Melisa ran to get it. People were talking, milling around, eating and drinking. The men were handing around the football.

There were about ten presents of various sizes on the coffee table in the living room. Iris was moving to open them when Melisa came out of the kitchen with the phone.

"Grandpa, it's for you," she said. "It's your cousin or something."

Lieberman took the phone, covering his open ear with his right hand and moving toward the bedroom.

"Lieberman," he said.

"Lieberman here, too."

There was no mistaking the voice.

"Senator."

"Detective. Am I calling at a bad time?"

"No, we're having a wedding party for my partner."

"He a Libertarian, too?"

"No, he's a Democrat."

"Maybe I should talk to him. Can you give me some more information on this fund-raiser?"

Abe gave him the information. The senator listened, spoke, asked a few more questions, and ended the conversation saying, "Maybe we are related."

"I've just concluded that anything is possible."

Lieberman stood for a few seconds, moved into the kitchen, and hung up the phone. Then he went back into the noisy living room.

"Was that Ernie in Cleveland?" Maish asked. "If it was our cousin Ernie, I wanted to talk to him."

Lieberman moved over to Bess, who took his arm.

"Who was it?" she asked.

"Senator Joseph Lieberman," said Abe. "He's going to be in Chicago for three days in July. If we're flexible, he'll come to a breakfast fund-raiser."

"This is one of your jokes, Avrum," Bess said. "It's not getting you out of cleaning the garage."

"I've got a number and the name of a woman to call in his office to set it up," said Abe, showing her his open notebook.

"They'll throw a dinner in your honor at the temple," Bess said.

"I'll settle for being retired from the fund-raising committee."

"Retired? They'll probably want you to be permanent chairman."

She kissed him on the cheek.

"So, do I get a reward?"

"What do you have in mind?"

"A moderate to large slice of the wedding cake Terrell is about to bring out of the kitchen. A moderate to large slice without looks of recrimination and arrows of guilt and betrayal."

"Granted," said Bess.

"Ladies and gentlemen," Lieberman said aloud, "I have a greeting for Bill and Iris. That was Senator Joe Lieberman on the phone."

Everyone laughed.

"It's true," said Bess.

Everyone stopped laughing, and Lieberman reached for a glass of wine set up with others on the sideboard. He lifted his glass and said, "From the groom's partner and the senator from Connecticut, *mazel tov.*"